Praise for Colm &

Shortlisted for the Bisto Book of the Year Award 2010

Colm & the Lazarus Key from Kieran Mark Crowley heralds a serious new player in the Irish fiction market for children ... Moves effortlessly between laugh-out-loud comedy and hide behind the sofa scariness. Three concurrent plot-lines, each equally engaging.

Inis Magazine

A funny, laugh-out-loud book.

The Irish Examiner

A lively fantasy adventure.

Irish Independent

A cracking debut novel.

Books Ireland

A rip-roaring adventure story ... a real page turner.

Verbal Magazine

Kieran Mark Crowley

Colm & The Ghost's Revenge

MERCIER PRESS
IRISH PUBLISHER – IRISH STORY

MERCIER PRESS

Cork

www.mercierpress.ie

© Kieran Mark Crowley, 2012

ISBN: 978 1 85635 997 9

10 9 8 7 6 5 4 3 2 1

A CIP record for this title is available from the British Library

Printed and bound in the EU.

For Adam

and for Jessica, Isobel, Cormac, Hugh, JJ and Luke.

Special thanks to the Borrisoleigh Aunties, a terrifying force of nature,

and to all my cousins spying in the bookshops.

The Book of Dread

My name is Colm. I'm eleven years old and I live on the northside of Dublin. As I write this, it's two in the morning and the city is asleep. Except for those who love the night, burglars and me. I don't sleep much any more. When I do, the things I dream about are terrible. But I'm not writing this to tell you about my nightmares. These words are to warn someone who may one day be as unlucky as I was. For those of you who think your lives are normal and boring and that there's nothing exciting out there for you, you're wrong. There is. And if you're not careful it will kill you.

There are only ten people in the world who know what I know. Two of them are dead. Of the survivors, one refuses to talk to me, the location of some of the others is unknown and the remainder live at least three thousand miles away. If someone had told me six weeks ago that I would be writing about strange and disturbing events for an ancient journal I would have thought they were mad. Now I think that I might be the one who's mad. I can hardly believe what I've been through. When I first read 'The Book of Dread' I was shocked by the tale the author told. I never imagined that I would be the one to write the next chapter of this horrible book. But I have no choice. It's my destiny.

All that happened seems unreal now that I'm here in my bedroom, surrounded by my books and games and clothes. Everything looks the same as it always did. I hear my mother snoring in the room next door, my father getting up to go to the toilet for the second time tonight. It's all so familiar and on the surface life goes on as it always has. Sleep. Eat. School. Homework. But in my head, the world has changed.

Eighty-three days ago The Incident occurred. The thing that changed my life. It began when my parents, myself and my cousin

Michael (I call him The Brute) decided to stay in the Red House Hotel, an old country house in the middle of nowhere. And when I say nowhere, I mean nowhere. You couldn't even hear a car passing it was so far from the main road, and it was surrounded by this huge, dark forest, so thick that it hid the hotel from the rest of the world. We were the only guests staying there. I won't lie – it was creepy. The only other people around were the owner, a cranky old woman called Mrs McMahon, her daughter Marie, Marie's American daughter Lauryn (The Brute kind of went weird when he was around her) and their friend, the tall, thin Professor Drake.

I found 'The Book of Dread' when I was nosing around the hotel library. When I saw it for the first time, I felt like the book was calling out to me, as if it wanted to be read. I couldn't help myself. I reached for it, but just as my fingers brushed its spine, Lauryn showed up and said that the book was cursed and anyone who touched it died within twenty-four hours. When I heard that, I pretended I hadn't gone near it and that everything was cool, but to be honest, it freaked me out. I really didn't want to die. Especially when there was still a week left of the summer holidays. Of course afterwards, when I thought about it, the whole idea of it seemed stupid. Why would anyone keep a book that killed people in the library of a hotel? Half the guests would be dead before the weekend was over. That would have to be bad for business.

I found out afterwards that Lauryn had made up the story about the book being cursed. She just wanted to get me and my family out of there as quickly as possible because the hotel contained a much darker secret than a cursed book. She didn't realise it would take more than the possible death of his only child to scare my dad away. He's not the most generous man - if you got my pocket money you'd understand - and since he'd already paid for the rooms, there was no way we weren't going to stay in that hotel for the night, even if we found out that all the staff were axe-wielding, child-hating maniacs.

The secret Lauryn was trying to protect us from was a mystical object called the Lazarus Key. There was a guy who had lived in the hotel about a million years ago. His name was Hugh DeLancey-O'Brien. Turns out he'd stolen this Lazarus Key (it wasn't literally a key, it was a diamond with a tiny skull inside) from a secret society in Boston back in the 1800s. The key was supposed to give the person who held it eternal life, but only if it was used correctly. Of course old Hugh didn't have the instruction manual, so instead of living happily ever after he ended up half-dead in a tomb buried deep in the forest. He must have been there for over a century, barely moving, his body decaying, his brain turning to mush, just waiting for a victim to come along and steal the key. That's what he wanted. You see, whoever took the key would give their life force to DeLancey-O'Brien.

He'd steal their youth and they'd end up all withered and dead while he'd be young again. Everyone was safe as long as they stayed away from the tomb. Of course, then The Brute went barging into the forest, found the tomb and took the key. Nice one, Brute.

So now we had this zombie creature coming after us, which was scary enough, but then we found out that this really tough criminal – number one on the FBI's Most Wanted List – was after the key too. This guy was so devious, so fiendishly clever, that no one knew his real identity. Even the FBI called him The Ghost. To cut a long story short, after some kidnapping (my parents), followed by some more kidnapping (me and The Brute), I ended up with the key. It was awful. That little diamond made my blood run cold. It made me weak and sick and brought me closer to death than I want to be for at least another seventy years.

Later, after escaping, I managed to trick

The Ghost into swallowing the Lazarus Key. The key was destroyed and the creature that was once Hugh DeLancey-O'Brien, who also almost killed me (it was that sort of night), wasn't able to survive in the sunlight. It died thanks to the help of an overweight man who mysteriously turned up in the middle of everything with his girlfriend. The man said their names were Bill and Jill and that they were tourists, but I didn't believe him. I think they must have had something to do with the key.

Now you know my story. Since then I have spent every spare moment researching the key, so that anyone who reads this book can protect themselves if a similar thing ever happens to them. This is what I have learned so far:

1. There were originally three keys. One key has been destroyed. By me. Two remain. A single key can resurrect the dead by drawing the life from any living person who holds it in his or her hand. The

living person will end up in a coffin if
too much of the life force is taken, but
things can go badly wrong for the dead
person too. They can end up in a half-
life for hundreds of years. Especially
when the key isn't used properly. And no
one I've met seems to know how to use
it properly.

2. If the three keys are used together
   by one who understands the ancient
   ceremony known as Abbatage, then they
   will make the user immortal and almost
   unbelievably powerful. This requires
   all the keys and a willing participant.
   Can't think why anyone would want
   to participate in that kind of madness.
   Abbatage, I think, would be a very bad
   thing for humanity, so I'm glad there are
   only two keys left.

3. The remaining keys are believed to be in
   Eastern Europe and Asia, buried with some

ancient warriors who tried to become immortal, but messed things up and ended up being buried with their keys.

4. A key can be destroyed by hydrochloric acid (yeah, the stuff in your stomach). Some say that running water and ice can also have an impact on it, although when I tried that with the key I found it had no effect. Another tale explains that the power of the keys can be wrecked by someone who disrupts the Abbatage ceremony, but the interrupter will almost certainly die, which is why this solution doesn't seem to have been that popular.

5. There was once a vicious gang in Boston known as the Sign of Lazarus. I don't know if they still exist, but they worshipped the key and used the one they had to control the city. They were among the most ruthless people ever to walk the earth. You can recognise them

by their tattoos. Each one should have a skull inside a diamond shape inked either on the tip of a finger or the inside of an arm.

6. The dead can be commanded by the holder of the key, but if the holder uses it improperly he can become one of the drifting dead – alive only in the darkness. Light is his enemy, powerful UV light can destroy him.

7. If you ever hear anyone mention the Lazarus Key, then you should turn around and run away immediately. It is a horrible thing and will only ruin your life.

8. I'm serious. Run.

That's all I have to say. I hope no one will ever have to use this information. I hope that whoever reads this will think that I was just a boy with an overactive imagination. If they do then it means that the remaining keys have not surfaced and that the world is still safe. With luck, the man they called The Ghost will have been the last one ever to search for the key. Since he is dead hopefully no one smarter will come after it.

•◆•

It has been over a year since I wrote those words and everything has been quiet and boring. Until today. I found this in a newspaper my father was reading across the breakfast table:

The robbery of the priceless Destiny Diamond bore all the hallmarks of the man whose true identity is unknown to those in law enforcement. Some call him the 'Napoleon of Crime', but most, including the FBI, know him simply as The Ghost. It was believed that The Ghost had perished in a freak accident in Ireland eighteen months ago, but a spokesman for the FBI today revealed that there have been developments recently which suggested that the dead man may, in fact, have only been an accomplice of the master criminal. The spokesman also admitted that they are no closer to apprehending him than they have been at any time in the last twenty years. The Ghost is believed to be responsible for over two hundred high-profile robberies and the deaths of forty-seven people, in addition to the disappearance of seventy-nine others, who are presumed to be dead.

If the real Ghost is still alive, then the rat-faced criminal who died in the woods probably just worked for him. I'm sure The Ghost won't come here though. Why would he? The Lazarus Key was destroyed. But if he does come, I hope he doesn't cross my path. Or yours. By the time you know it's him it will be too late for you to save yourself, so there is no point worrying about what he might do.

But I'm still scared.

One

Fintan Wickerly was a deeply unpleasant man who had grown increasingly mean with every passing day. He had been a postman for twenty-seven years and he'd hated every single second of it. So had the people who'd been unfortunate enough to have their letters and packages delivered by him. And the neighbourhood pets weren't exactly fond of him either. Especially the dogs. In an unusual turn of events, the dogs on Fintan's route were afraid of the postman. There was something about the man that transformed them from happy-go-lucky cat botherers into twitching, nervous wrecks. It wasn't just the angry set of his jaw, his booming voice or his general rudeness. It was more than that. They seemed to sense that he was someone you should keep away from. Not a single dog had ever bared its teeth or dared to bark at Fintan. It was unheard of for one of them to growl when he was within a fifty metre radius. As for nipping at his ankles, well, only a pooch with a serious death wish would consider that.

Every morning, when they heard the squeak of his bicycle wheel or the hacking sound as he cleared his throat and spat on the ground, most of them would run around the back of their owner's house and cower there until he'd left. Others would hide under cars, duck beneath a hedge, or, in the case of Nigel, an elderly springer spaniel, stand completely still and hope the postman would mistake him for an extremely lifelike statue.

Of course, it wasn't just animals that had a problem with Fintan Wickerly. His fellow postmen weren't happy at having to spend time with him either. They said that to know him was to hate him, and it was true. Everyone hated him, even his own mother, and let's be honest, you have to be a spectacularly horrible person to be despised by your own mammy. Fintan had often been surprised to discover Mother Wickerly wasn't at home when he called to borrow some money and drop off his dirty washing. Especially since she was eighty-three-and-a-half years old, particularly feeble and very, very rarely left the house. He didn't realise that every time he banged his fist on the red front door and shouted her name she actually *was* at home. Just like the dogs, she hid too. She'd throw herself from her wheelchair onto the carpet, then crawl on her wrinkled, blue-veined hands and arthritic knees until finally she was behind the couch and out of sight. She'd rather risk months in hospital with two broken hips than spend a single second of the remaining years of her life in the company of her boorish son.

Luckily for his mother, Fintan Wickerly wasn't anywhere near her home on the day his rental car rattled twice, belched an enormous plume of black smoke and spluttered to a stop.

He was deep in the heart of America.

More specifically, he was on a little dirt road that wound its way through a forest which sat in the shadow of the magnificent Blue Ridge Mountains – a little dirt road that earlier in the journey he'd hoped would take him to Lynchburg, but which now appeared to lead to the middle of nowhere. He popped the bonnet with a sigh, got out of the car and stared at the engine. When that didn't fix things, he gave up. He felt like kicking something, preferably something small and furry, but there was nothing fitting that description within reach of his foot so he kicked the wheel instead. That was a mistake. Pain shot through his big toe (which had been home to a particularly nasty bunion since the morning of his forty-sixth birthday) and he hopped around for a while swearing inventively until the agony faded into mild discomfort.

It was turning into a really rotten holiday.

All he'd wanted to do was to drive a car around America for a month. A road trip like he'd seen in the movies. He'd planned to eat in diners. Wear a cowboy hat. Watch baseball. Stay in motels. Cut across the country and see Hollywood. But things hadn't gone according to plan. His airline had accidentally sent his luggage to Azerbaijan. The Ford Mustang convertible he'd booked hadn't been available and he'd been given a little yellow hatchback as a replacement. He'd lost his mobile phone after a fight in a biker bar. And now this. Why did his car have to break down? And if it had to do so, why did it have to be here, just as it was beginning to get dark? The dark in America wasn't like the dark in Ireland. There were dangerous things out there.

'Why do bad things always happen to good people like me?' he shouted in frustration as the rain which had been threatening all afternoon began to fall. Fat drops rolled down his neck and under the collar of his Munster rugby shirt. He got back into the driver's seat and waited there, listening to the radio, hoping that someone would eventually see him and stop to help fix his car.

Waiting and listening.

As the rain pounded on the car.

And no truck or car passed by.

Waiting and listening.

As darkness fell.

And the night took hold.

And still no vehicle passed by.

Until finally, the car's battery died.

And Fintan Wickerly began to worry.

It was time to make a decision. He was either going to spend the night freezing in the car with no blankets or food – and his stomach had already begun to rumble

— or else he was going to have to get out and seek some other form of shelter. He couldn't remember passing a house in the last few kilometres of his journey, but there had to be one somewhere up ahead, hadn't there? They don't just build roads to nowhere, he told himself, as he climbed out of the car for the second and last time.

·◆·

Fintan had been striding down the middle of the road, as purposefully as his bunion would allow, for what felt like hours and he still hadn't come across any sign of civilisation. Without a torch or the moon to guide him, he'd occasionally wandered off the track, but then his eyes had adjusted to the night and he'd become more confident. For a while. The purposeful striding was downgraded to a hearty walk and then a sullen trudge as tiredness began to take hold. The rain eased off, not that he cared very much. He was already soaked through. He knew he needed to find shelter quickly. He was wondering how long it would take to die of hypothermia when he heard a howl coming from the woods.

'Probably longer than it would take to be eaten by a wild animal,' he muttered.

He wasn't sure what sort of creature could produce such a howl. A coyote? A cougar? A bear? Did bears even howl? It hardly mattered. What was important was whether or not he could outrun any of them if they caught his scent. He was a forty-seven-year-old burger-loving postman and whatever lurked in the night was a wild animal that survived because of its speed, strength and stealth. The odds weren't exactly stacked in his favour.

Then he saw a light up ahead. A tiny pinprick in the distance, but a light all the same. He felt adrenaline surge through his body. His legs and arms might not be ripped off after all. He might live. He picked up the pace. Another hundred metres farther on and he could see a blurry, dark shape beneath the light. A contrast to the trees. Was it a house? He was almost sprinting now, his bunion pain a distant memory. No sign of any creature from the woods either. Half a kilometre later and Fintan Wickerly smiled for the first time in six months. It was a house. Of sorts. More like a cabin.

Sweet relief.

Surely whoever was in there couldn't refuse him shelter. Even if they did, Fintan decided that it wouldn't stop him. He was going in there no matter what they said. They could give him a meal. And a bed for the night. A hot shower would be nice too. Yes, he'd be their guest. They'd have to treat him right. He left the road, cut through the trees and up a slight incline until he reached the log cabin. It was pretty basic and probably charming in some sort of rustic way, but he didn't care. All he wanted was some place safe. A refuge from nature. He pounded on the door with his fists.

No answer.

The rain started up again, splattering onto the dirt path that had been made by successive footprints. He tried the handle. To his surprise the thumb latch clicked. He pushed the door open.

'Hello,' he called out.

There was no reply. The cabin was small and not very well decorated, but all he focused on were the orange flames flickering in the stone fireplace, bathing the room in a warm, welcoming glow.

'Hello,' he shouted again. 'My car broke down and I need to use your phone. I'm coming in.'

Still no reply. He stepped inside. Ah, he thought, the heat's the job. He crossed the room, rubbed his hands together and warmed them by the fire before easing himself into the armchair with a satisfied grunt. He slipped out of his shoes, peeled off his stinking socks and laid them on the hearth to dry.

He took another look around the room. Now that he noticed it, there weren't any homely touches: no flowers or plants, no paintings or photos, nothing to indicate the owner had any family or friends. Just like me, Wickerly thought. He didn't have friends because he thought most people were boring eejits and why would you want to waste your life hanging out with boring eejits?

As for his family, well, most of them hadn't spoken to him since he'd tripped over a poorly positioned nephew in his sister's house and broken his leg. They'd got annoyed with him just because he'd sued them. Why shouldn't I have sued them, he thought. Stupid child lying in the middle of the floor drooling like a puppy. He'd won the case and the compensation money they'd been forced to give him had paid for his holiday to America. Of course, it also meant his sister and her husband had to sell their house to pay the legal bills, and now there were seven of them living in a rented two-bedroom flat, but that'd teach them to control their children rather than let them run wild around the place like a congress of baboons.

When his feet were toasty and the rest of him had dried out, he decided it was time to locate a telephone and a directory. He had to find a mechanic if he was going to get his car sorted and get back to his holiday. There was another reason too. Even though he wouldn't admit it to anyone, and didn't want to admit it to himself, there was a gnawing feeling of doubt at the back of his mind. The bravado he'd felt when he first arrived was fading. Maybe being here wasn't the greatest idea he'd ever had. The owner would be back soon if that fire was anything to go by, and even though any reasonable person wouldn't mind someone in trouble warming themselves by the fire, perhaps the owner wasn't a reasonable person. And this was America, not Ireland. They had guns here. Guns were scary. Especially in the hands of an unreasonable person. Yes, better hurry and find that phone.

He began to search the small cabin. Nothing in the kitchen. No phone in the bedroom. Or the bathroom, which was a good thing. It'd be terribly unhygienic.

He turned the place upside down, but he still failed to unearth a phone. And the gnawing feeling grew stronger.

Think, Fintan, he told himself. There might not be a phone, but there had to be a computer. Everyone has a computer these days. He could get in touch with someone on the Internet and they could help him. The only thing was that there was no sign of a computer either. Aha, Fintan thought, clearly on a roll, if the man has a laptop he may have hidden it to prevent it from being stolen. Now where would you hide a laptop?

After a further ten minutes of searching, he thought he'd found it at the back of the kitchen dresser, hidden behind the cereal boxes. But he was wrong. It wasn't a laptop. It was a long, thin wooden box with gold trim on the edges. It was held closed by a small brass clasp. No padlock though. Wickerly unhooked the clasp with his thumbnail and opened the box. His mouth dropped open when he saw what it contained. I've got to get out of here now, his mind screamed, as his legs buckled under him. He grabbed the dresser and steadied himself. This was bad. This was really bad. He was in so much trouble his mind was unable to take it all in.

'I see Goldilocks hasn't aged well.'

Fintan's eyes widened in surprise when he heard the velvet voice of the man who was standing behind him. If he hadn't opened them to their maximum potential at that particular moment, he'd have opened them even wider when he turned and saw the two dogs flanking the man. Rhodesian Ridgebacks. Like every good postman, Fintan Wickerly knew his dogs. This breed was big and strong, with a distinctive stripe on its back. Ridgebacks had often been used in South Africa to hunt lions. Fintan Wickerly may have been many things, but a lion wasn't one of them. And he knew just by looking at them that, unlike the dogs back home, these two weren't afraid of him.

He gulped. 'I … I …'

The dogs bared their teeth and growled. Low and menacing. Fintan's shoulders tightened and he felt knots of tension popping up at the base of his skull. He dearly wished he'd stayed in the car.

'Easy, Keyser. Stand down, Moriarty,' the man whispered.

The dogs stopped growling immediately and sat back on their haunches. Wickerly said a silent prayer of thanks.

The man standing before him was tall and pale, his

smooth skin almost white enough to be transparent. He was also good-looking, but in that too perfect way that gives you the creeps rather than drawing looks of admiration. There was something too symmetrical about his face. No flaw to draw the eye and make him seem human.

'You broke into my home,' the man said.

His voice was still calm, Wickerly noted. Too calm. Most people coming home and finding a man going through their stuff would either be terrified or furious. This man wasn't either. A shiver decided to take a jog along Fintan's spine.

'Ahm, it's like this – my car broke down and I lost my phone and it was raining and I was looking for somewhere to shelter. I didn't know the place was occupied.'

'I would have thought the fire in the hearth was a clear sign that someone was staying here,' the man said, his tone only slightly south of freezing.

'Yes, I, ah, what I meant to say was that I would ...' Fintan realised the sentence had nowhere to go. 'I don't want any trouble,' he added.

'I don't care what you want,' the man said, brushing a

stray lock of hair from his forehead. He moved towards the wooden box. 'What did you see?'

His body language was unreadable. Fintan wondered how he should play this. Apologise? Act tough? It would all depend on whether the man was angry, amused, bemused or concerned.

'Me? I saw nothing.'

The man's eyes suddenly burned with fury. Right, Fintan thought, it's anger then.

'Tell me.'

'Or what?' Fintan asked aggressively. When all else fails, try bluster.

'They won't find your body, you know. A single, middle-aged man. From the south of Ireland judging by your accent. A farmer? No, the hands are too soft. But you do work outdoors, you have a ruddy complexion. A postman, perhaps? Three thousand miles from home. On holiday by himself. That means no family or friends. Nobody who'd care that much anyway. You're someone who can be disposed of very easily.'

Fintan knew he'd stepped into the wrong house at the wrong time. That was very clear now. It was just a pity it hadn't become clear before the arrival of the terrifying man and the dogs with the crazy eyes. He decided that it would be best for him to do exactly what the man said. That way there might be a chance of surviving the night. A slim chance, but that was better than no chance at all. A million times better.

One of the dogs leaned forward and nuzzled his leg with its wet snout. He could feel its hot breath on the back of his knee. So this is what genuine terror feels like, he thought.

'I saw a name. And … the thing. The … erm … objects.'

'What name did you see?' the man asked.

'An Irish name. I … it seemed unusual. Here of all places.'

'Don't make me ask this question a third time. What was the name?'

'Colm,' said Fintan Wickerly.

'Who sent you here?' the man asked.

'No one. I wasn't lying. My car broke down.'

'Then you're just very, very unlucky,' said the man they called The Ghost.

TWO

The library was quieter than usual for a Saturday morning, but Colm didn't mind. It suited him. He nodded hello to Mrs Dillon, the friendly librarian, then followed up with a 'hi' to Edan, the local genealogy expert, who was sitting in his usual spot surrounded by a pile of books and sheaves of papers. He passed by the old people who were poring over the daily newspapers, occasionally raising their heads to comment on the state of the world, and took his place at one of the computers, quickly getting to work.

Two hours later he leaned back and yawned, rubbing his tired eyes. The monitor was a blur. He hadn't uncovered any new information on The Ghost or the Lazarus Keys, so he'd moved on to researching the working methods of the great detectives: Holmes, Marple, Rockford. He hoped that they might give him some idea of how to proceed with his investigation. He was aware that his interest in the master criminal and the supernatural keys was turning into an obsession, if it wasn't one already, but he didn't know how to stop it. All his other interests had fallen away and he'd grown distant with the few friends he had. He wanted to explain his situation to them, but he couldn't. Having people think he was weird was one thing, allowing them to believe he was mad was another. Thinking about the situation put him in a foul humour, just as it always did.

He was only supposed to have been on the Net for thirty minutes, but when there wasn't anyone waiting a turn Mrs Dillon allowed him to stay on the computer well past the allotted time.

'How are you, Colm?' she asked, leaning over his shoulder. Her hair smelled of peaches and cream.

'Good thanks, Mrs D,' he replied, too polite to mention his bad mood. 'Can I get a print-out of these pages?' he asked waving his hand in the general direction of the computer.

'Of course. How's the book going?'

Ah, the big lie. Colm had been coming to the library every Saturday morning for the last eighteen months and over that time Mrs Dillon had become increasingly chatty. One day, she'd asked him what he was working on. He didn't want to tell her the truth. It would have sounded ridiculous. So he'd told her that he was doing research for a book he was planning to write. Of course, if you want to keep a librarian off your back, telling them you're writing a book isn't the way to go. Books are like catnip to them. It led to a serious amount of questions, which in turn led to Colm having to make up the plot of a story which he had to relay to Mrs Dillon on a monthly basis. After that, every time he went in she would go out of her way to help him. It made him feel very, very guilty.

She printed out the pages he'd asked for, Colm handed over the money, and a couple of minutes later he was out on the street and back in the real world. Unfortunately. The city was sprinkled with the light of the fading sun. Colm swung his bag over his shoulder and headed for the bus stop. The streets were crowded, filled with the hum of conversation and the stop-start of passing traffic.

Colm heard Ziggy before he saw him. His voice rose above the crowd: loud and braying and American, even though Ziggy wasn't from America; he was born and bred in Dublin. He'd never even visited the US, but he spoke with the accent because he thought it fitted in with his image. To be fair, it did, since his image was that of a Californian surfer. Still, Ziggy didn't surf and the opportunities for wearing the baggy shorts he favoured were quite limited in the less than tropical temperatures in Ireland, unless you were a fan of goose bumps.

He was a neighbour and classmate of Colm's, and lived on the far side of the estate. Only two hundred and four steps away, as Ziggy had once informed the class.

'What's the difference between the coolest guy in the universe and a chubby-faced mammy's boy?' he'd asked. 'Two hundred and four steps,' he'd said, pointing at Colm.

Their fathers had worked in the same factory before it had closed down and Colm's mother was always encouraging Colm to hang out with Ziggy, as she'd recently decided that what he needed was a new friend.

She didn't know what a pain their neighbour was since he was one of those kids who makes sure they are always friendly and polite when adults are around, their nastiness only emerging when the adults leave the room.

For once, Colm was glad of Ziggy's inability to speak in a tone lower than booming. Being alerted to his presence meant he could avoid him. He wasn't in the mood for whatever sarcastic zinger Ziggy would send his way. He could see him clearly now, hanging out in front of the chip shop with Iano, the best friend Colm always suspected that Ziggy secretly hated because he was funnier and more popular. Amy was there too. And Stephanie. The 'A1 Crew', as they called themselves.

Time to disappear, Colm thought. He crossed the street, waving apologetically to the man on the bicycle who was forced to weave around him. When he was on the far side he glanced back to see if the crew had seen him. That was a mistake.

'You stepped on me toes, ya chipmunk-cheeked moron.'

Oops.

In his desire to see if he was in the clear, he hadn't

noticed the three teenagers leaning against the shop front. All of them were dressed in football shirts and tracksuit bottoms as if it was some kind of uniform. Buzzer, Killer and Neil. Three guys with nothing to do and all day to do it.

'Sorry,' Colm said.

The teenagers weren't having that. Colm felt a thump on his shoulder. In the past he would have put his head down and walked away because he knew that they wanted him to react, just to have a reason to start a fight. The smart thing to do was to ignore the punch. And Colm was smart.

Usually, that is. Not today though. Today he'd had enough of all the lies and having to keep his fears bottled up. He felt like a pressure cooker that was about to explode.

He shifted his gaze so that his eyes met those of the guy who was acting like the leader. Buzzer stared back, not even blinking once. His sidekicks stopped slouching. This wasn't going the way it normally did. It had just got interesting.

He's going to ask you a question, the sensible part of Colm thought. He wants an excuse to beat you up and no matter what you say he's going to pretend it's an insult. Don't give him the ammunition.

'What're you looking at?' Buzzer asked.

'An eejit with an enormous nose and a tiny brain,' Colm found himself replying.

I'm dead, he thought as soon as the words left his mouth.

It took Buzzer a full five seconds before what Colm had said registered. He couldn't believe this fat little kid had said that and his brain was frantically checking to see if there was another, more respectful, way of interpreting the words.

During the time it took Buzzer to process the insult, Colm's sudden rush of anger died and he remembered that there were three of them and one of him. But even if there were ten of him and only one of them he'd probably still get his butt kicked. So he used the rest of the time that Buzzer's brain was grinding into action to take off. He sprinted down the footpath, followed by the words he really didn't want to hear.

'Get him!'

·◆·

POLICE REPORT   No. 213486
Date: October 9th
Department: Olde City, Philadelphia
Incident: Missing Persons
Case Number: OL/PH/AQ/98982
Reporting Officer: Detective Adam Quigley

At approximately 21.40 on October 8th, I arrived at the home of Professor Peter Drake in response to a call I had received from a neighbor of his, Mrs Kovicek. She said that she had not seen Drake, his girlfriend or his girlfriend's daughter in almost a week. She claims to be on good terms with the family and that they usually inform her when they are going away for even short periods of time.

Upon arrival I found the back door swinging open.

I proceeded into the house as Mrs Kovicek had barged in ahead of me, in contravention of my warning not to set foot inside the property, and I was compelled to follow to protect her from any possible intruders.

There were none. I found no direct evidence that any crime had been committed. Two plates of half-eaten food sat upon the kitchen table. Professor Drake's cell phone was in the living room with twelve missed calls. The television was still on, but there was no sign of the family. It was as if they had just disappeared. There one moment, gone the next. The people who are listed as living in the house, but who are now believed to be missing, are as follows:

Professor Peter Drake, aged 52 years

Marie McMahon, aged 37 years

Lauryn McMahon, aged 16 years

Three

As Colm reached the end of the shopping area, dodging people left and right, the crowd began to thin out. Nobody raised a finger to help him though. They were quick enough when it came to getting out of his way, but it was clear that they didn't want to get involved. It wasn't as if they didn't know what was going on either – you didn't need to be an expert in body language to understand the meaning of a twelve-year-old boy with terror written all over his face racing down the street pursued by three teenagers waving their fists and shouting threats.

'You're a dead man,' one of the trio roared.

Colm wanted to provide a witty comeback, but his heart was pounding, his throat was dry and scratchy and, to be honest, the only reply that came to mind was: Technically, I'm not even a teenager yet, so calling me a dead *man* is a bit dumb. No, it was better to focus on getting away from them than trying and failing to be clever.

The running-in-a-straight-line-along-the-street plan wasn't proving to be as successful as Colm had hoped. In fact, it was failing quite badly. The teenagers were within arm's length now. He could hear their snorts and ragged breathing. Colm had to do something. He veered to his right and ducked into an alleyway. His pursuers weren't expecting it and flew past, still on the main street. The detour had only given him a few extra seconds and he needed to … it was a dead end. He swore silently and came to a halt.

At the far end of the alley stood an imposing eight-foot wall. Unless he developed superpowers in the next couple of minutes there was no way he was going to be able to scale *that*. He had to face the truth. He was trapped. He scanned the alley again, this time looking for somewhere to hide. The only thing large enough to provide any kind of cover was a faded green plastic wheelie bin. Slime oozed gently down the sides and a trickle of rubbish juice dripped from one of the handles. It wasn't particularly appealing.

'I'm going to kill ya, ya little son of a maggot,' Buzzer announced as he arrived in the alleyway.

Right, Colm told himself, it's time to fight. It wasn't really a decision he'd come to through some brilliant and original thinking. When you're trapped in an alley and the guy who wants to beat the bejeepers out of you is standing less than two metres away, you either have to fight or else just stand there and let him punch you repeatedly until he tires himself out. Being a punchbag wasn't Colm's thing. Trouble was, fighting wasn't his thing either.

He'd begun taking karate lessons at a club on Collins Avenue a few months previously. He thought it might be helpful to know some self-defence moves if he ever found himself in a dangerous situation again, but the karate hadn't really worked out for him. In fact, 'it hadn't really worked out for him' was a huge understatement. It had been a disaster. He just wasn't good at sports. Whichever part of his brain was responsible for co-ordination seemed to have been wired wrong. When the instructor had told them to move left, he'd found himself going right. He punched when he should have kicked and kicked when he should have punched. It was like swimming against a roaring tide.

His third and final lesson had been the straw that broke the camel's back. The instructor, a man with enormous biceps, a deep voice and worryingly hairy ears that captured your gaze like a hypnotist's pocket watch, liked to roar his commands in Japanese. This was a little odd as he wasn't from Japan; he was a Navan man through and through. He'd even played corner back for the Meath minors. But if he wanted to speak Japanese then no one was going to tell him he shouldn't. Would you argue with a man who could put you in hospital before you could say the words 'fractured coccyx'?

I didn't think so.

The thing was, Colm wasn't great with languages so when the instructor had shouted 'Bow' in his Navan-Japanese accent, he'd mistaken it for 'Kick'. He'd attempted an ungainly roundhouse just at the moment Seamus Barry had begun to lean forward and unfortunately for Colm, and poor Seamus, he'd caught him right on the bridge of the nose. There was a tremendous crack followed by a brief moment of silence. Two seconds later, Seamus was slumped on the sparring mat with blood and tears pouring down his face. It was agreed by the instructor, Colm's parents, Seamus's folks and a couple of people who had no business interfering, that it might be best for everyone concerned if Colm tried a different sport.

'Hey, Killer. Neil. Is that kid just standing there thinkin'?' Buzzer asked, puzzled by the blank look on Colm's face and the lengthy passage of time that had elapsed since he'd issued his threat.

'Looks like it,' Killer agreed.

'He's disrespectin' ya, Buzzer,' Neil said, egging him on. Neil loved nothing more than watching someone being beaten up.

Buzzer sighed. This day was proving to be very unusual. Was it too much to ask for things to go smoothly? All he'd wanted to do was find a wimpy little guy, beat him up, then go for a bag of chips. And what happens instead? He gets insulted, has to chase the kid all over town, and then the kid blanks him. Why is life never easy, he wondered. Well, it was time for the messing to stop.

Killer and Neil exchanged glances. Now Buzzer was

at this thinking thing. Was it contagious?

'Hey Balloon Butt, are ya going to spend all bleedin' day standin' around thinking with a stupid look on yer face or are ya going to fight like a man?' Buzzer asked, snapping out of his reverie.

'Two things,' Colm began. 'One, I'm a couple of weeks away from my thirteenth birthday, so technically I'm not a man.' Nope, still not a good line. 'And number two ...'

'Huh, huh. He said number two,' Killer chuckled.

And that's when Colm attacked. He launched himself at them, fists out front, face set to DESTROY. Unfortunately, his ability to fly through the air didn't quite match his ambition. In less than a tenth of a second it was clear his unexpected move was doomed to failure. He landed at Buzzer's feet a full metre short of his target, cracking his chin on the cobblestones. He looked up, his face a picture of despair.

Buzzer peered down. It seemed like he was going to say something, but was holding back for some reason. His lip began to wobble. He sniggered. Then he started laughing. Long and loud. Killer and Neil joined in, because that's the kind of lackeys they were.

'Aw, man,' Buzzer spluttered, wiping away the tears. 'That's the funniest thing I've ever seen. The way ... you thought you could ... pat'etic.' He mimicked Colm diving through the air. 'It's a bleedin' classic.'

'So you're not going to hurt me because I made you laugh?' Colm asked, his voice crackling with hope, his jaw sore and tender.

Buzzer extended a hand and hauled Colm to his feet.

'Nah, kid, we're not goin' ta hurt ya,' he said.

Well, Colm thought, when he was up to his shoulders in rotting food and dirty nappies, it could have been worse. Buzzer had been as good as his word. They hadn't hurt him. All they'd done was dump him in the wheelie bin. Upside down. It had been quite stomach-churning at first, but he'd got used to the smell and the waves of nausea more quickly than he'd expected once he'd righted himself. His bag of library notes was in pretty poor shape though.

He wiped some semi-solid sour milk from the face of his watch. The ten minutes they'd told him to stay inside the bin were almost up. It had been one really bad day. At least I've learned a valuable lesson, he thought, trying to look on the bright side, which, when you're sitting in the dark in a wheelie bin with six days' worth of other people's rubbish soaking through your socks and shoes, is something that requires a glass-half-full mentality.

'Isn't that right?' Colm said to the black rat that was scrabbling its way up his trouser leg.

The rat stopped at the sound of Colm's voice. It looked at him and swished its long tail, waiting for the boy to explain what lesson he'd learned. But Colm didn't elaborate. He just looked at the fat-bellied rodent and sighed.

Four

The moment Kate Finkle opened the front door of her flat she knew something was wrong. It wasn't the torn newspapers on the floor, the blaring TV or the half-empty cans of cat food lying on their side on her threadbare two-seater couch; her flat was exactly as she had left it. No, what set off the alarm bells in her head was the fact that Mr Gilchrist, her favourite cat, didn't immediately leap from whichever corner he was hiding in and wrap himself around her ankles, as he did every single evening when she returned home.

Kate wasn't your average person. For one thing, she worked as an assistant to a private detective, the much disliked Cedric Murphy. For another, she was a large woman who took no pride in her appearance. Make-up, new clothes, dyeing her hair, none of these things meant anything to Kate. They took up too much time, time she would rather spend working or tending to her cats and goldfish (to be fair, the goldfish didn't need much minding, but the cats were a demanding lot). She loved being tall and heavy. It intimidated people and intimidating people was fun for Kate. Especially when someone was acting the fool. One glare from her and they'd shut up. She couldn't charm the birds from the trees, but she could certainly scare them off the branches.

She stepped over the empty crisp packets and into the living room just as the man who had been hiding behind the sofa stood up. He was thin and wiry and the scars on his face told of previous battles.

'Prepare to die,' he said.

That was his first mistake. Kate Finkle grabbed him by the collar and lifted him into the air until his feet dangled six inches above the bright blue carpet. He kicked wildly against her shins, but if this bothered her, she didn't show it.

'What have you done to my cats?' she roared. It wasn't the time for diplomacy.

The man took a swing at her, but Kate's reach was longer than his and his fist didn't even brush the tip of her nose. She slammed him against the living room wall and heard the air leave his body with a little whoomph sound.

'Your cats are safe in the bathroom,' the man spluttered, wondering if his ribs were broken in two or three places.

'Lucky for you. Who are you and what are you doing in my flat? I've got nothing that's worth robbing,' she said. This was true. Even the telly – a portable – was worth less than fifty euro and it was the most expensive item she owned.

'I'm tellin' you nuthin',' the man replied.

Kate lifted him higher. His hair brushed against the ceiling.

'Mammy,' the man whimpered.

Two thoughts went through his head simultaneously. The first was that Kate was far more frightening in person than in the photos he'd been given. The second was that he was glad he'd brought along two accomplices.

Kate sensed the men before she saw them. She

swung around, the wiry man still in her ferocious grip. The thugs were standing on the far side of the living room, less than ten feet away. Both were huge, bald, ugly and dressed in black.

'Hello boys. Aren't you great for dressing up like twins. You look really cute,' Kate sneered.

The slightly prettier of the two smiled, revealing a mouthful of broken, yellow, rotting teeth.

'Whoa, they should put your picture on bars of chocolate as a warning. No kid would ever want to eat sweets again if they thought they'd end up looking like you.'

The men didn't say anything. They just took a step towards her. Uggo cracked his knuckles. Pretty Boy took out a police baton. Uh-oh, thought Kate, you had to antagonise them, didn't you. She tried to take a step backwards but the wall was blocking her way. Her options were limited.

'Let me down,' said the man. He was still dangling in the air and had grown quite embarrassed about it. His accomplices would be mocking him about this one for months.

Kate sized up the situation. Three against one. She

was good, but not that good. What would Cedric do in this situation, she wondered. There was only one thing for it.

'Let me down. I won't ask you again, *Kate*,' the man said.

Calling her Kate was his second mistake.

Using her free hand she grabbed the wiry man by his belt buckle and hoisted him above her head in a move she'd seen Randy Orton use in a WWE match.

'It's Miss Finkle to you, ya stick insect,' she shouted, flinging him at the thugs. He sailed through the air accompanied by a tiny yelp. The men swiftly moved out of the way, making no effort to catch their colleague. He landed face first in a dish of soggy day-old cat food.

Kate didn't wait to see what happened next. She turned and sprinted for the front door as quickly as she could. It wasn't quick enough.

Before her hand had reached the latch, the thugs were upon her. In less than three seconds she was unconscious.

Five

'In the name of all that's good and holy, what's that smell?' Colm's mother cried, flapping her hand furiously in front of her face.

Colm closed the front door, took off his shoes and popped his head round the kitchen door.

'I think, Mary, that that insufferably awful stink is our one and only child,' his father replied.

'Hi Ma. What's up, Da?' Colm asked in as cheery a voice as he could muster.

The journey home had been mortifying. The driver wouldn't allow him on the bus – 'Janey, son, were ya showering in sewage or wha'?' – so he'd had to walk. A real walk of shame. Fellow pedestrians had given him a wide berth. Most had given him odd looks. More than a few had tried to be smart alecks – they'd made jokes about slurry and Stig of the Dump; one wag had told him to familiarise himself with a substance called soap that had existed for roughly five thousand years. A Yorkshire terrier had even sniffed at Colm's shoes, before running off into the distance leaving behind an auditory trail of high-pitched whimpering, possibly traumatised for life by the appalling stench. It wasn't Colm's finest hour.

'What happened to you?' his dad asked, his face a mixture of concern and amusement.

'I fell,' Colm replied.

His father arched an eyebrow. 'It must have been a spectacular fall.'

Why did he have to say he fell? He was fed up with secrets and lies. He'd kept the events of *that* night from his parents. And his friends. He was lying to Mrs Dillon. It was getting too much for him. All it did was make him feel guilty.

'Colm, your father's talking to you.'

'Huh?' Colm snapped out of his daydream.

'Don't say huh, say pardon,' his mother said.

'Pardon?'

'I said, we have to go to Maynooth at the weekend to collect a second-hand engine I found online.'

Ah yes, the engine for their little red car that had broken down. Again. Everyone else agreed it had broken down because it was fifteen years old, had over one hundred thousand miles on the clock (not bad for its age – Colm's dad wasn't much of a driver), and that its time was up. Everyone except Colm's father, that is.

'I thought you said you hadn't the money to fix it,' Colm said.

His father had been unemployed until very recently. He had worked in a factory, but shortly after it had been bought by new owners it had suddenly been closed down, much to everyone's surprise. The following six months had been tough as money was very tight, but then, out of the blue, his dad had got a job as a night watchman in the newish shopping centre on the edge of the city, even though he'd never worked in security before.

Colm's father switched on the radio, which, as always, tuned into some old geezer's station. An ancient song from the eighties or nineties squeaked through the tinny speakers and suddenly he grabbed his wife and began to twirl her around the kitchen.

They weaved their way past the stools, their stockinged feet gliding silently over the faded lino.

It was at moments like this – moments which were far too frequent for his liking – that Colm wished he had a brother or sister. Just so there was someone to share the embarrassment with. He didn't mind seeing his parents happy, but this was taking it too far. Next thing they'd be ... yep, there it was: the kiss. Not just a peck on the cheek or a quick smackeroo on the lips either. It was sloppy and wet and horrible.

I think I'm going to puke, Colm thought. 'Uh, that's disgusting. You're all old and wrinkly. And ... and ... you're my parents. And you're kissing. Eeeurgh. Can you cut it out, please!'

They ignored him, so Colm focused his gaze on the kitchen clock which seemed to be ticking by slower than if he was stuck in a double Maths class.

'What was that for?' his mam asked her husband when she finally came up for air.

'I should have told you earlier, but I wanted to wait until we were all here. I've been promoted. Head of Security. I'll be in charge of the whole centre and responsible for twenty-two staff.'

'Does it mean more money?'

'A twenty-five percent pay rise,' his dad replied.

'Weeeeaaaaaahhhhhh,' she screamed. She was trying to say three different things all at once and it came out like some kind of horrific wail, but the gist of it was that she was thrilled. When the screaming subsided the two of them began jumping around in circles and high-fiving each other.

'C'mon, son,' his mam said, extending her hand for Colm to join in the celebrations.

'Can't. Still all stinky,' Colm said, glad to have an excuse. 'I'm going for a shower.'

Wheeeeee, they continued as he left the room. It didn't look like they were going to stop any time soon.

He felt better after the piping hot shower. Much better. And his odour was far less offensive to the nose. He was squeaky clean and fresh, and felt a lot more like himself. He got dressed in his fleece hoodie and his favourite pair of slightly faded jeans. It was good to be warm and cosy again. He put on his glasses, bringing the world back into focus, then stuffed his rotten clothes into the laundry basket for his mother to deal with later.

Back in his small room, he reached under the bed and pulled out the big black folder that held all his notes. He thumbed through the pages, occasionally taking one out and reading over it again. This was something he'd done hundreds of times now; he almost knew all the pages off by heart at this stage. Sometimes he thought he was probably the world's foremost expert on the Lazarus Keys. Well, him and Professor Peter Drake. Not that anyone cared, except for the occasional weirdo on a supernatural website.

He was distracted by the smell wafting up the stairs. A good smell this time – something frying. Something mouth-watering. His stomach reminded him of how hungry he was and he shoved the notes back in their folder and under the bed before racing downstairs, two steps at a time, skipping over the squeaky third step. His mother was by the cooker, humming to herself, but his dad had disappeared.

'Take a seat, love,' she said without turning around.

Colm did as he was told. The kitchen table was laid out for one person. A fizzing glass of cola sat to the right of the knife and fork, alongside the salt, vinegar and ketchup.

'I hope you're hungry,' his mother said as she carried the plate to the table. Double cheeseburger and chips. Homemade chips. This was a treat. The chips were thick, golden and crispy. The burgers were big and juicy, the bun filled with fried onions, two slices of melting cheese, beef tomatoes and crunchy iceberg lettuce. And there was a portion of curried beans on a side plate. He hadn't had a meal like this in ages, not since his dad was working overtime at the factory. Then it hit him. It was a bribe of some sort. It had to be.

'Why are you being nice to me?' he asked.

'What? I'm always nice to you.'

Colm raised an eyebrow.

'All right. It's because we're celebrating your father's promotion. Is that a bad thing?'

'No. Sorry, Ma. I just ...'

'You're grand, Colm. Just eat up.'

He tucked in. Her cheeseburger and chips was even tastier than he remembered. It took all of his willpower not to wolf the entire lot down in one go. Boy, it was delicious. He stuffed seven chips into his mouth. It was one too many and one of the smaller ones popped back out and landed on his plate, a little soggier than it had started out.

'Glad to see you're enjoying it,' she said, tousling his hair.

It was the tousling of his hair that confirmed his suspicions. His mam was always giving out to him for stuffing too much food into his mouth at once. He should have been rewarded with a smack across the back of the head, not a sign of affection. She was up to something all right.

'Ma?'

'Hmmm?'

'Did you know about Dad getting the promotion before me?'

'No, Colm. He wanted us both to find out at the same time. Don't you remember him saying that?'

'Yeah.'

He paused for a moment. His mother's moods had been a bit changeable recently and he didn't want to say the wrong thing and set her off. Especially when he hadn't finished his dinner. There was a possibility that she could throw it in the bin. Still, he had to say what was on his mind.

'You just cooked my favourite meal, but you didn't have to go to the shop to get the ingredients. That means you had them already,' he said.

'So what?'

'It's my *favourite meal*. Why would you have been cooking this for me when you didn't know we had something to celebrate?'

His mother looked as if she was holding back a swear word.

'And why am I eating alone? Why aren't you having something?' Colm continued.

'A mother can't be nice to her son without him getting all suspicious? What kind of world are we living in? You've hurt my feelings now,' his mother replied, turning away. She sniffed, then wiped her eye with the knuckle of her index finger, as if she was brushing away a tear.

'Too much, Ma,' Colm said.

'What?' his mother said.

'Pretending to cry. Really? Come on, you don't cry over stuff like that.'

'OK, you caught me,' she sighed. 'I need a favour.'

She wasn't telling him he had to do something. She

was asking a favour. This was dangerous territory. Colm knew he had to be careful. His mother could be cleverer than a fox with a Harvard degree when it came to things like this.

'What is it?'

'Nothing much. Just a little thing.'

'Ma?'

'Your dad's gone to work. Night shift.'

'Yeah.'

'But I'd already made plans to go over to Lisa's.'

'Oh. That's it? That's OK. I don't mind hanging out here by myself.'

'Nope. I trust you, but you're not staying at home on your own.'

Colm's mind flicked through the pages of the book of possibilities. What could she mean? Surely, she wouldn't get somebody to babysit him? Not at his age. That'd be embarrassing. Rachel did all the babysitting around the estate and she was only fourteen. Not even a full two years older than him.

'There's a party,' his mother said.

'What? A party? Lisa's having a party?' Then it hit him. His fork clattered to the floor. 'Oh no. No way.'

'You don't even know what I'm talking about yet.'

'I know exactly what you're talking about. Is it a birthday party?'

She nodded.

'A birthday party for a boy on the other side of the estate?'

She nodded again.

'You want me to go to Ziggy's party?' He shook his head vigorously enough to cause a slight dizzy spell. 'Not a hope, Ma.'

'Colm ...'

'No, I'm not going and there's nothing you can do about it.'

Of course there was plenty she could do about it. She could withhold affection, food, pocket money; give him nothing but unfashionable clothes to wear; make him do all the cleaning and tidying in the house. And that was just for starters. Let's face it, he was twelve years old and entirely dependent on her for everything. Well, wait until you're old and you need someone to push you around in a wheelchair, Colm thought. We'll see how you like it when I'm in charge.

'Just tell me why I have to go,' he said in the end. He

was too tired to argue or run up to his room and sulk. It had been a very long day.

'It'll do you good,' she said.

He knew she wanted to say more and he knew what that was too. She'd been worried about him. Worried that he was spending so much time on his own, that since the night at the Red House Hotel he'd lost the few friends he'd once had. She thought it had something to do with his dad being on the dole or that he was going through some sort of pre-teenage mood swings. She hadn't a clue what the real reason was.

'Ma, Ziggy's a dope and there's no way I'm going to his party. No matter what you say or what you do, I'm staying here.'

'Colm,' his mother said in the icy tone she reserved for moments like this.

'Right. What time am I supposed to be there?' he asked, caving in immediately.

Six

The man they called The Ghost had slipped into Ireland unnoticed several days ago, ever the master of disguise. He lit up a cigarillo and took a long drag, exhaling a series of smoke rings, then rubbed the palm of his left hand over his newly shaven head. It felt odd, being hairless. He watched from a hill high above the car park as the men struggled to move the wooden boxes into the building. Men who had never seen him. Men who didn't even know they were working for him. If they did they might have been more concerned for their health, for everyone in the criminal underworld had heard the horrible tales of what became of the men who worked for The Ghost. But they would still have done their jobs. Those who refused suffered an even worse fate.

'You always were a loner.'

If The Ghost was surprised by the voice of his dead brother, his face didn't show it. He turned his head slightly to get a look at the rat-faced man. He wasn't much to look at, just a shell now. A rotten shell.

'I know what you're thinking – am I real?' the rat-faced man said.

'You never knew what I was thinking, not when you were alive and certainly not now that you're dead,' The Ghost said in his smooth, velvety voice.

'You'd be surprised at what I know.' The rat-faced man surveyed the scene below. 'I know that you're taking revenge for my unfortunate death.'

'Your foolish death.'

'I was tricked,' the rat-faced man said, irked. 'That fat little child threw the Lazarus Key into my mouth and the creature took me.'

'If I were you I wouldn't admit to anyone I'd been tricked by a child,' said The Ghost, crushing the butt of his cigarillo beneath the sole of his brown leather boot. 'And I wouldn't be so certain that revenge was my only aim.'

'I know that. I know a lot more now. You see things more clearly when you're dead.'

'How interesting,' The Ghost said wearily.

'You're not just seeking revenge. You're trying to save yourself too. You're dying.'

'We're all dying.' The Ghost almost smiled. Almost. He didn't like any display of emotion. That was for the weak. And The Ghost wasn't weak. He never had been. He had vanquished every foe. Except one. Death. The rat-faced man was right about that. He was dying. He had only weeks left. Unless his plan succeeded.

'You're going to try the Abbatage ritual. Make yourself immortal. Yet you never showed any interest in the keys before, any interest in immortality.'

The Ghost didn't say a word.

'But you can't do the ritual. You need the three keys. Two have been missing for hundreds of years and the one I swallowed was destroyed.'

'Was it?'

The rat-faced man seemed confused for a moment. Then it dawned on him.

'No!'

His spectral hands lifted his shirt and revealed his

belly. His white belly with a long red scar. 'You cut me open and took the key.'

'What's left of it.'

'You desecrated your own brother's body?'

'By saving myself I will also avenge your death,' said The Ghost.

'But you need the participant to be willing,' said the rat-faced man, still staring at the jagged scar.

'He will be willing,' said The Ghost. 'I will have the keys soon and he will do what I say. He will save me whether he wants to or not.'

·◆·

The only reason the proprietor of the Scimbleshanks Bed & Breakfast was still alive was because she reminded McGrue of his mother. If it hadn't been for that unremarkable fact, in that all grey-haired old ladies look the same to the casual observer, she'd have been as dead as a dodo, a dinosaur or any dead thing you'd care to think of. When he'd arrived the previous evening, the first thing that had annoyed him was that the proprietor wasn't actually named Scimbleshanks, which was a terrible disappointment. Unbeknownst to him, the name had been chosen as pure whimsy after a literary festival reading of a T. S. Eliot poem. The second thing that annoyed him was when she refused to accept that his name was McGrue.

'What kind of name is that?' the woman had asked.

She was filling in the little registration card which wasn't necessary, but was a habit she'd got into when she'd run her own hotel, and this woman was someone who never broke a habit she'd formed.

'*My* name,' McGrue said gruffly.

'Hmmmph. What's your Christian name then?'

McGrue wasn't a Christian, but he presumed she meant his first name.

'Don't have one.'

The woman had snorted in disbelief. 'Don't be stupid. Everyone has a Christian name. What is it?'

McGrue did have a first name, but it had been thirty years since anyone had last used it. To be honest, there were moments when he couldn't even remember it himself. Even his mother called him McGrue.

He kept his temper. It wasn't easy.

'Just put down McGrue,' he said.

'So your name is McGrue McGrue,' the woman

muttered, writing it down on the little card she used on such occasions. 'Americans,' she muttered under her breath, thinking that her strange new guest wouldn't hear her.

He did hear her. He had better hearing than anyone he'd ever met and was quite proud of the fact. The woman led him up the floral carpeted stairs and into the hideously decorated room that would serve as his base for the night.

'Breakfast is from eight to ten. If you're out late then take off your shoes when you come in. Don't want you waking the house,' she said, handing him a key.

'What about dinner?'

'It's a bed and breakfast. The clue's in the title,' the woman replied sharply before softening a little. 'You can get something to eat in Snook's, the pub in the village.'

He grunted his thanks as she left, then locked the door. He hefted his suitcase onto the bed and unzipped it. All it contained was a change of clothes, a cardboard folder, a selection of weapons and a photo of his mother.

McGrue loved his mother more than he loved life itself, although since he wasn't a huge fan of being alive, that wasn't saying much. However, it was true to say that he adored her. She was the one who had made him what he was – the best bounty hunter in the country. She had told him to quit school when he was fourteen. She had bought him his very first gun, made him get his first tattoo and paid for his Krav Maga self-defence lessons.

He had been a bounty hunter in California for twenty-two years and was considered the best in the business, both by himself and others. He was married to the job. He had been married to a woman once, but his wife had left him after either five or six years. McGrue was never quite sure which it was, as he hadn't been home for six months when he'd found out she'd left him, and since she hadn't dated the note she'd left – which had read, 'I hate you. Don't look for me because you won't find me. Goodbye' – he wasn't sure how long she'd been gone.

He had found her, working as a waitress in a dingy bar in Cleveland, Ohio. She looked shocked when she arrived at a table to find her husband sitting there, but all he said was: 'Don't tell the best bounty hunter in the business that he can't find you. It took me seventeen hours and twenty-four minutes, honey.' Then he'd walked out the door and never seen her again.

He had retired six months ago, but then he found his mother was unable to take care of herself any longer and he wasn't very good domestically. He'd made the decision to put her in a nursing home. Not just any old home either, the most expensive one in the country. After three months his savings had been spent, so he decided to take some freelance work. It paid better, especially when you worked for criminals. It didn't sit easy with him, working for the people who he'd once spent all his time trying to put in jail, but he did it for his mother. This new job was something unexpected though. The pay was exceptional for one thing. It'd pay for three years in the nursing home. All he had to do was find some people in a small country.

McGrue swept his greasy hair into a ponytail, then opened up the cardboard folder that The Ghost had sent to him. A sheaf of A4 papers with descriptions and details of their day-to-day lives. It was more thorough than any file he'd ever been given. It even told him what their favourite breakfast cereals were. At the back of the papers were two photos. One was of a young, slightly tubby child of twelve whose name was Colm. The other was of an older child, the boy's cousin. His name was Michael.

All McGrue had to do was grab them and deliver them to a specified location if the other people who were tracking them failed. Do that and his mother's lodgings would be secure for the next thirty-six months. He wasn't too happy about the idea of delivering children into the clutches of a man who had to be up to no good, but what happened to them after he had done his job wasn't his problem, he reasoned, dismissing any feelings of guilt that might have been bubbling under the surface. No, it was just another job to be done. A conscience wasn't something you needed as a bounty hunter – he'd leave the agonising about right and wrong to priests and philosophers. However, he hoped that when he found them they wouldn't put up a fight. He didn't want to hurt them, but if he needed to then he would. He wouldn't hesitate for a second.

Seven

Number 64 Sea View Crescent was the second to last house in a narrow cul de sac that afforded a view of the sea only to those with access to an extension ladder and a pair of binoculars. Even though it was on the far side of the green, Ziggy's house was almost identical to Colm's: an uninspiring, faded-yellow, semi-detached home with a narrow strip of grass in the front. All the houses on the estate — and there were hundreds — were yellow and practically indistinguishable from one another, which made it difficult for any visitors to find the house they were looking for, especially since local vandals had taken to twisting the road signs until they pointed in the wrong direction. Pizza delivery men and women could often be seen driving aimlessly around the roads of the Riverwood estate with a haunted look in their eyes and rapidly cooling pizzas in the back of their cars.

Colm stood on the doorstep, a present under his arm, his finger poised above the silver doorbell. He'd been there for ten minutes wondering whether or not he should press it. If he did, then that'd be it, he'd be spending the next few hours in Ziggy's lair. It wasn't that he hated Ziggy or anything. Hate was far too strong a word. They didn't get along. Nothing wrong with that. People have different personalities. We can't all be friends.

Actually, he thought, changing his mind, I do hate him. Quite a lot.

He could see the party through the frosted glass of the front door. Kids running up and down the stairs, shouting wildly. Knowing he'd regret it later, he finally pressed the doorbell. Ziggy's face appeared at the glass almost instantly. He was the kind of person who was easily recognisable even when his face was slightly blurred.

'Who is it?' he called out in his fake American accent.

I can see you, Ziggy, you can see me, and even if you couldn't, all you would have to do is open the door and have a look, is what Colm thought. But all he said was, 'It's me. Colm.'

Ziggy sighed loudly. Colm was the last person he wanted to see. He'd only wanted cool people to come to his party and Colm wasn't cool. Neither was Ziggy for that matter, but he believed he was and that was enough for him.

'Muuum, that stoopid kid from across the green is at the door. Why did you invite him?' he yelled.

Nothing like a warm welcome, eh? The door swung open. Ziggy was still dressed in his surfer uniform. His hair was shaved at the sides and what remained was gelled into a diagonal mohawk. He could have been an escapee from a Nickelodeon sitcom. He looked at Colm like he was something he'd stepped in.

'Hey,' he said without enthusiasm.

Great, Colm thought. He's doing his teenage rebel thing. Did he even realise that rebels don't have birthday parties hosted by their mammies? What a jerk.

A boy of four or five who looked like a miniature version of Ziggy ran towards Colm waving a silver baseball bat in the air. Without warning, he took a wild swing, cracking the aluminium bat right against Colm's shin.

'Holy sh–' Colm began, then bit his lip. The pain was excruciating. He hobbled around trying to walk it off. He wondered if it would be bad manners to give the kid a kick when his leg had recovered. Probably.

'That's my brother, George,' Ziggy said. 'You can leave the present on the hall table.'

He ran upstairs. Back to where the party was going on.

Colm rubbed his leg furiously. Man alive, it really stung. He turned up the leg of his jeans and examined the injury. A huge red welt was beginning to form. Out of the corner of his eye he spotted George preparing for another swing, a smirk playing on his pink lips.

That kid's properly mental, Colm thought. He dodged to his left as the bat arced towards his exposed shin, missing it by centimetres. It smacked off the front door, leaving a dent in the PVC.

George burst into tears when he saw that his mission had failed and that the new party-goer wasn't lying on the floor screaming in agony as he'd hoped. It was so unfair.

'Waaaaaah,' he cried and legged it into the kitchen as quickly as his spindly little pins would carry him. His mother emerged moments later, marching furiously towards Colm.

'What did you do to George?' she asked.

'N-n-nothing,' Colm said.

She leaned in until they were almost nose to nose.

'He's only five you know. What sort of boy picks on someone who's only five?'

'I didn't pick on ...'

She put her arm around George's shoulders. 'The poor child is terrified. Look at his little face.'

George didn't look terrified. He stuck out his tongue.

'I've a good mind to call your mother and ask her to take you home right this second,' she spluttered.

Please do, Colm thought. He'd only been here for ninety seconds or so and already it was the worst birthday party he'd ever attended.

'Well?' said Ziggy's mother.

Colm looked at her. She seemed to be waiting for him to say something.

'I'm waiting for your apology,' she said.

Apologise? No way, he thought. She glared at him.

He tried glaring back at her, but found that when it came to glaring he really wasn't very good at it. He noticed that her make-up was heavily piled on and while her face was dark and had an unnatural brown tinge to it, her neck was porcelain white.

'Sorry,' he muttered.

'Hmmpph,' Ziggy's mother replied and disappeared back into the kitchen.

'You stink like smelly poo,' George said, and ran off to join her.

•◆•

George's baseball bat attack was the high point of the party for Colm. He spent the rest of the time being ignored by all the guests, most of whom he knew from school or the estate.

He ended up in a corner of the kitchen eating bowl after bowl of the tasteless nachos no one else wanted to touch while Ziggy's grandmother sat beside him telling him her life story. She was a nice lady, but it wasn't as if she'd spent her life trekking to the North Pole or living with gorillas; she'd worked in a shop for forty-seven years and had never been on an aeroplane.

When the food had been demolished and everyone had half-heartedly sung Happy Birthday (Iano replacing the standard words with rude ones) Ziggy's mother got to her feet.

'Right, everyone. Into the living room for a game of charades.'

There was a chorus of disapproval.

'Muuum. We're not playing charades,' Ziggy wailed. Colm had to admit that Ziggy had got this wailing thing down pat.

'What's wrong with charades? I used to love that game when I was young.'

'Back in the 1800s,' somebody whispered.

'What do you want to play so, Jonathan?' she asked, using Ziggy's real name, which sounded odd because even the teachers didn't use it any more.

'Anything that involves you leaving us alone,' he replied.

'OK, love. You lot get out while Granny and me clear up.'

The fourteen party-goers squeezed into the small living room – some on the couch, others on the arms and seats of the leather chairs. Those who weren't quick enough to find a perch ended up on the floor. Colm was one of them. When they'd all settled down, Ziggy lit a large white candle and placed it in the centre of the coffee table, then switched off the main light. The candle's flame flickered. A girl giggled nervously.

'What are we going to do?' she asked.

'We're going to tell ghost stories,' Ziggy replied.

Eight

Cedric Murphy, the private detective, sighed as he ripped open the white envelope. Another bill. He took a look at the figure at the bottom of the page. He owed them how much? He felt like he'd been punched in the gut by a man with rocks for fists. He crumpled up the paper and threw it across the room where it bounced once before rolling gently into the pile of sixteen other scrunched-up bills that sat beside the wastepaper basket. Murphy's cramped flat now doubled as his office and the neatness and orderliness that had once been an important part of his life were long gone.

He took a slice of cold pizza from the takeaway box and wondered if it was safe to eat. It hadn't been in the fridge since he'd bought it the previous night and the two dead flies stuck in the congealed cheese made it a little unappealing. He picked them out and wolfed down the pizza before thoughts of bacteria, gut-wrenching illnesses and days spent on the toilet had fully formed in his barely awake brain. Cedric's head hurt, his hair was a mess and he hadn't slept in almost three days. He wasn't even sure if it was morning or night and he couldn't summon up enough energy to open the curtains and find out. He scratched his enormous belly, broke wind, then frowned as he caught his reflection in the mirror. Was that really him? He wondered how he had let himself get so out of shape.

Eighteen months ago, when the rat-faced little man had engaged his services for the oddest case in all his years of detective work, Cedric had been so frightened he'd promised himself that if he got out of the situation alive he'd go on a major diet. He had too. For a while. Green tea and porridge for breakfast. Cabbage soup for lunch. Brown rice and vegetables for dinner. It was vile. He'd lost weight, plenty of it, but he was always hungry. Always. Thin people didn't really know what true hunger was, he thought. It gnawed at you constantly.

Your stomach growled, begging to be fed a tasty morsel, preferably something made from fat or sugar. He was almost at the point where he was imagining other people as steaks or hamburgers like they did in cartoons.

And the headaches. No one had told him about the headaches he'd get when he began dieting. It was as if Woody Woodpecker had taken up residence in his skull and invited all of his raucous woodpecker friends around for a wild house party.

Sure, Cedric looked better, felt better too eventually, but there was always a tiny voice in his head telling him to have one teensy little biscuit. And a slightly larger voice in his office telling him to eat one too. His assistant, Kate Finkle, was constantly nagging him to eat, eat, eat. Not because she didn't want him to be slim – secretly, she found him rather attractive that way – but because when he was dieting he was the crabbiest, most contrary man on the planet.

They had always bickered and both had enjoyed it, but when he lost the weight Cedric had become downright obnoxious. If someone said black, Cedric wouldn't just say white, he'd say, 'Shut your mouth or I'll wipe that stupid look off your pig-ugly face. Moron.' He was ruder than he'd ever been and he wasn't someone who'd ever been known for his good manners and sociable ways.

There was a low point which convinced Cedric that dieting wasn't for him. Someone had cut in front of him in a supermarket queue and he'd lost it. He'd been overcome by a complete Berserker fury. He'd roared and shouted at the woman who'd skipped ahead before finally emptying an entire carton of buttermilk over her head. Buttermilk didn't flow easily and it took a good thirty seconds for the carton to empty over the nun. She didn't like having to wipe it from her eyes or the front of her jumper and Cedric had to make a large donation to a convent school to avoid getting in further trouble for that one.

That was when he'd decided to start eating properly again. And now he couldn't stop. It's not my fault, he told himself. Business had been bad for the last year. Actually, bad was a bit on the optimistic side. Atrocious was more accurate. At first he'd thought it was due to the recession – people weren't that concerned about what their wives or husbands or employees were up to when they were worried about their jobs and homes. But the recession should have only caused a small loss of business. This was different. It was a catastrophic collapse. One minute he'd been bobbing along nicely, fewer clients, but still enough to pay the bills, next minute, boom. Nothing. Not one client. Not a single person had walked through the door in the last six months. The bills had piled up, the bank savings had dried up and Cedric knew that this week he was going to have to tell Kate Finkle she didn't have a job any more. She would no longer be his assistant. Poor Kate. That job was her life. He wondered how she'd take the news. Probably by breaking my nose, he thought.

Of course, being a detective, he'd tried to discover the cause of this loss of business. He'd found it too. A new detective agency had opened up. A rival. Just around the corner. And they only charged one-tenth of the price. Now, even those who don't know much about business could see that that just didn't add up. No detective firm could charge so little and hope to stay in business. And there wasn't enough room in Dublin for very many detective agencies as it was, never mind two in the same area. No, he was sure that the only reason they were doing it was because they hoped to drive him out of business and as soon as he closed down they'd up their prices. It was an old business trick and, as far as Cedric was concerned, an extremely sneaky one.

He thought it would be best for the owner of the new business and him to have a nice little chat, man to man. Then, when the chat was over, he'd threaten his rival. His plan was that they'd be so scared they'd immediately close down and then everything would go back to normal.

It hadn't gone exactly as he'd hoped. Not even close. He'd called to their office, ready to speak to whomever was in charge. He'd even had a speech prepared. He'd opened the door to The Ark Security Agency and announced to the receptionist, 'I'm Cedric Murphy.' Four seconds later a muscle-bound ape in a tight black t-shirt had picked him up, carried him out of the office and thrown him down the stairs. He'd had better meetings, but it was a mark of Cedric Murphy's character that he'd had worse too.

Going back to see them a second time would have been foolish and stubborn, adjectives which most people who knew him would use in a description of

Cedric. So he did go back. This time he received a few digs and elbows before he was thrown down the stairs.

On his third visit, he was met by two goons with guns. Cedric Murphy didn't mind getting a few punches or kicks. They came with the territory. And bruises faded, broken bones healed. Bullets though? He had a problem with bullets. Especially ones that could cause him to suffer a severe case of death. He smiled his most charming smile.

'Don't worry about it, lads,' he'd said. 'I'll save you the trouble.'

He threw himself down the stairs.

As he lay in a crumpled heap, his leg twisted in a way likely to induce a fit of vomiting in anyone who saw it, Cedric realised that he was going to have to try a different approach if he was going to save his business. He also realised, as the blinding pain surged through his ankle, that he'd really begun to loathe the inventor of stairs.

The Ark Security Agency then stepped up their attack on his business. They weren't subtle. They posted a man in the hall that led to Cedric's office. Any time one of Cedric's potential clients arrived to unveil their tale of woe they found themselves confronted by a man who'd politely hand them a card for The Ark and explain that their prices were ninety percent cheaper than Cedric's and their offices were nicer, cleaner and only around the corner. And you'd get a free coffee and a doughnut even if you decided not to avail of their services. The free coffee and doughnut swung it for most people.

Those clients of Cedric's who decided to remain loyal to him were dealt with less politely. Let's just say they didn't make it to his office. The employees of The Ark began to intercept Cedric's phone calls and emails and told the people who rang or mailed that they couldn't trust a detective who allowed himself to be monitored in such a manner. And one by one the clients left, until he had none.

Cedric grabbed an ice-cold can of cola from the fridge, slumped onto the couch and gulped it down. It felt good and gave his brain the kick-start it needed. He had no clients, no proper office, very little money and a car that was in dire need of a service. Was he going to lie back on his couch and watch episodes of sitcoms he'd seen a million times already or was he going to get off his ass and do some work? He had to admit the sitcom idea was a tempting one. It would offer a temporary escape from his troubles, but when he turned off the TV later the troubles would still be there waiting for him. No, he had to fight back. He looked at the sheets of data lying on the table. Facts and figures about The Ark. He hated paperwork. It was useful and possibly the most important part of his job, but he hadn't become a detective to spend his time sitting around an office. He needed to be Out There. In the world.

The little black gadget in his pocket beeped once. He took it out, looked at the screen and allowed himself the tiniest of smiles.

Yesterday, while the man who was guarding his stairs had thought Cedric was in his new 'office', he'd actually been attaching a tracking device to the man's car.

They were on the move. If they were up to something he'd find out by following them. He put on a shirt, gobbled another slice of pizza and pocketed his car keys.

'You have no idea who you're dealing with, boys,' he said to himself, puffing out his chest in pride.

The problem for Cedric was that he had no idea who he was dealing with either. If he had, he'd have just gone back to bed and hidden under the covers.

Nine

'It's nearly Hallowe'en, dudes,' Ziggy began.

'Are we going to bob for apples? 'Cos I can't do that. It'll ruin my make-up,' Amy said. She was the most popular girl in Colm's class. She thought she was far more beautiful than she actually was and most of the time she acted as if anyone who spoke to her was lucky to be allowed to share the same air.

'No,' Ziggy sighed. 'We're not going to bob for apples. I just said we were going to tell ghost stories.'

'I wasn't listening,' Amy admitted. She had been checking her reflection in a glass cabinet.

'Nothing too scary, I hope,' Stephanie said.

Scary is kind of the point of a ghost story, Colm thought.

'The gruesomer the better,' Iano said, desperately hoping his bravery would somehow impress Amy. 'Lots of blood and gore and murder and stuff.'

'Eeeeeewwww. Stop,' Stephanie cried.

Colm glanced at his watch, which he noticed was still streaked with dried-up sour milk. How much longer before he could leave without it being considered rude? Twenty minutes?

'I'll start,' Ziggy said.

He moved to the centre of the room. The candle flame cast shadows on his face. He lowered his voice until it was almost a whisper. People leaned in closer to hear him.

'OK,' he began. 'This story is true, right. It happened to my cousin's best friend's brother a couple of years ago.'

When he was sure he had everyone's complete attention, he continued.

'It was a dark and stormy night and ... Johnny was driving home from the cinema with his girlfriend. He was tired and he wasn't paying attention to the road. He ended up taking a wrong turn onto a country lane. Full of potholes and cow dung and stuff like that. He realised they'd gone wrong, so he decided to turn back. But the road was really narrow and he couldn't find a place to swing the car round, so he started turning left and right and back and forward and long story short ...'

'Not that short,' Iano whispered.

'They got stuck,' Ziggy continued. 'Now, all this time his girlfriend was moaning at him: "You're a muppet, Johnny", stuff like that. Johnny got annoyed and pressed his foot too hard on the accelerator. The car shot forward and rammed into a ditch. No matter what he did they couldn't get it out. They were trapped.'

'Why didn't they just ring their parents or the AA?' Amy said.

'Ahm, there was no mobile reception in the area, so they couldn't use their phones,' he said, thinking on his feet. 'Anyway, they sat there for ages and it got darker and darker, stormier and stormier, creepier and creepier. Next thing they heard a sound on the other side of the ditch. A strange metally sound.'

'How did they hear the sound if it was so loud and stormy?' a guy called Peter asked.

'They just did, right,' Ziggy said, getting a little hot under the collar. What was wrong with these people?

Couldn't they just listen to him? 'Oh, wait. I forgot a bit – they turned on the radio while they were waiting and they heard that a killer was on the loose. In the very area they were just after driving to.'

'How did they know what area that was if they'd taken a wrong turn?' Amy asked.

'I ...'

'Aw, man, I know this story,' Iano said before the host could offer yet another explanation. 'It's *The Hook*. Everybody knows it.'

Stephanie hadn't heard it before, but she was glad she didn't have to hear it now. Her hands had been trembling ever since Ziggy had switched off the light.

Ziggy's face had turned a colour a professional painter might describe as Scarlet Lake. In other words, quite red. 'Right,' he said. 'I've got another one.'

But that didn't work either. It turned out that Iano had heard nearly every ghost story ever told: *The Woman Hitchhiker*; *The Man Upstairs*; *The African Mask*; *The White Dog*. It almost drove Ziggy mad. He'd spent ages looking up stories on the Internet. He was going to pretend that they had all happened to people he knew, just to make them scarier, but none of that mattered now. Iano was ruining it, just so he could look good in front of Amy.

What a twonk.

'Well why don't you tell a story so, since you seem to know everything there is to know about ghosts,' he spluttered angrily after Iano had once again ruined the ending.

'I'm not a storyteller, man. I'm an athlete,' said Iano, flexing his weedy muscles, which caused Amy to explode with laughter. Cola shot from her nose and onto Ziggy's favourite shirt.

'Anyone else got a story? A true story?' he asked, wiping the snot-fizz from his chest and desperately trying to hold on to his temper. If he gave out to Amy, Iano would definitely have the upper hand with her. They'd probably end up dating, and even though Iano and Ziggy were supposed to be best friends, the last thing Ziggy wanted was for Iano to end up with the girl he fancied.

Stephanie looked in Colm's direction.

'What are you looking at *him* for?' Ziggy exploded. 'He's the most boring kid that ever lived. Five seconds in my world is more interesting than his whole life.'

'She can look at me if she wants,' Colm said. He was trying to stand up for Stephanie, but she didn't take it that way.

'I wasn't looking at you, weirdo,' she said. 'As if.'

'Yeah, seriously, Colm. No offence, but who'd look twice at you?' Amy said. She would have been surprised to know that Colm actually was offended.

'That *was* a stupid thing to say, Big C,' Iano added.

Colm wasn't going to take the bait and make some sarcastic remark, no matter how much they got under his skin. He was just going to get up, walk out of the room, go home and have a big bowl of cereal and watch whatever programme happened to be on the National Geographic channel. As he got to his feet, Ziggy stood up too.

'Where do you think you're going?' he asked.

'I'm going home,' Colm replied, heading towards the door.

'That's rude.'

'What?'

'Leaving my party before it's finished. Shows you've got no class. Shouldn't have expected any more of you anyway. You always wander around acting like you're better than all of us,' said Ziggy.

'You don't want me here,' Colm said calmly. 'I don't want to be here. It suits both of us if I leave.'

'What? I don't want you here, that's true. But you're lying when you say you don't want to be here. This is the coolest party ever. You were lucky to be invited. Nobody wanted you to come, you know,' Ziggy said, his voice getting a little higher with each passing sentence.

'I know nobody wants me here. And now I'm going.'

'Nobody leaves my party until I say they leave,' Ziggy squeaked.

That was it for Colm. He was sick of all of them. He was exhausted from keeping secrets and telling lies. He just wanted his life to be normal again. Something popped in his brain. It was the part of him that always remained polite. It was as if it was saying: I'm outta here, buddy, do whatever you like, say what you gotta say.

So Colm did.

'You know what? I hate your party. You lot think you're so fantastic, but all you ever do is judge other people, moan about haircuts and clothes, and sit around watching movies.'

'What makes you think you're so cool?' Iano sneered.

''Cos you're not. Far from it,' Amy added.

'I know I'm not cool, but so what? I'd rather be me than waste my time trying to impress someone so stupid that when our Maths test had a question asking us to "find x" he put a circle around it and wrote "there it is".'

'Anyone could have made that mistake,' Ziggy said defensively.

'And you can't even tell a simple scary story without getting it all wrong,' Colm continued.

'I suppose you could,' Amy said.

'Yes, I could, actually,' Colm said. 'And it'd be true too. None of this my mother's brother's friend's cousin's gardener stuff. It really happened to me.'

'What frightening story could you have? The day you wet your nappy?' Ziggy sneered.

'Yeah, and it was only two weeks ago,' Iano said to peals of laughter.

'The time the teacher got cross with him for forgetting his homework? That was really scary, wasn't it, Colin?' Stephanie said.

'It's real and it's terrifying and my name is Colm,' he shouted.

There was a sharp intake of breath from the entire group, followed by a deathly silence.

'Oooh, Mr Touchy,' someone whispered.

Colm could hardly believe what he was doing. Was he really going to tell them the truth he'd kept hidden from everyone for so long? The truth that had given him nightmares. The truth that had changed him, turned him into a different person.

Maybe it'd do him some good to get it off his chest. They all hated him anyway; they all thought he was a loser. It wasn't as if they were going to think less of him. He could hardly sink lower in their estimation.

They stared at him, with none of the hostility he'd expected. A sea of blank faces.

He opened his mouth to speak, but no words came out. Not a single one.

He couldn't tell them about that night. He just couldn't do it. Life at school was bad enough as it was with them just thinking he was a bit odd. If he started going on about supernatural events and zombies and cursed books … no, the secret would have to stay with him. Colm's heart sank. Why had he said he was going to tell them a horror story? He'd have to make one up now. What could he tell them? Nothing came to mind. When he'd stood there for thirty silent seconds, mouth open, but nothing coming out, they began to snigger.

'See, I told you he was an eejit,' Ziggy said to a boy who hadn't spoken during the entire time Colm had been at the party.

There wasn't any good explanation he could give them, no reason for standing there like a twonk, so Colm simply left the living room with the sound of harsh laughter echoing in his ears. He opened the front door and escaped into the night, gently pulling the door shut behind him. He was glad the estate was quiet for once. He didn't want to see anybody right now. He steadied himself on the front wall of Ziggy's house and took a deep gulp of cold air. His knees buckled. I almost told them, he said to himself. What had he been thinking?

Wrapped up in his thoughts, he failed to notice the dark figure watching him from beneath the solitary tree on the edge of the green as he began his walk home. Or the bounty hunter who'd been tracking his progress all evening. It wasn't as quiet out there as he thought it was. Far from it.

A big yellow moon hung over the estate. Colm

picked up the pace, trying to warm up. A rattling sound carried through the air like a whisper. He paused for a moment. Had he heard something? He was sure he had. He just didn't know what it was. He considered looking around, but he wasn't that far from his house. There were some dodgy characters living around here. People you didn't want to get on the wrong side of, or any side of for that matter. He wished he hadn't left Ziggy's so suddenly. His mother would kill him if she knew he was out on his own after dark, even so close to home.

He quickened his step until he was moving like a speed walker and in less than a minute he was home. He unlocked the front door, went in and shut the night outside where it belonged. Tomorrow'll be better, he said to himself. It had to be.

Boy, was he wrong.

Ten

They were some of the roughest, toughest, meanest men who had ever existed. Men with gold teeth and stubble sharp enough to cut glass. Men who ate with their fingers and considered a punch in the jaw to be a friendly greeting. Men who would sell their own mothers for the right price, even if that price was a Choc Ice and half a pack of cigarettes. The sort of people your parents warn you to stay well away from.

Mercenaries.

Dirty, low-down mercenaries. Thirteen faces, each uglier and more frightening than the last. Every one of the men had spent at least some of his life in prison; most for incidents involving broken teeth and shattered bones, some for crimes too horrible to even consider. And Jean-Paul Camus, the Sorbonne-educated man-about-town, had spent the last year and a half of his life working with them. Leading them. The stress had been unrelenting. It had given him a stomach ulcer that had been around for so long now he'd given it a name.

He called it Fred.

Camus pulled the collar of his waxed coat up around his ears. It didn't help. The coat was built to withstand the rain, but it was no match for this atrocious weather. He hadn't been warm in days and the wind was blowing a gale, even though none of the weather forecasts had predicted it. It was so windy that he could have sworn he'd seen a small dog spinning through the air only minutes previously.

But it wasn't the weather that was really bothering him, it was his location. A Gothic graveyard in deepest Transylvania. The crumbling headstones, the gargoyles at the broken-down entrance gates, the strange cries cutting through the darkness – the whole thing gave him the creeps and he wished he was anywhere other than where he was at the moment. He couldn't let the men know that, of course. The little bit of authority he had over them depended upon him remaining cool and calm in any situation.

The nasty and violent moneygrabbers from ten different countries stood around impatiently, waiting to be told what to do. They were on the verge of mutiny. The money he'd been given to pay them was good, exceptionally generous in fact, but they hadn't had a proper day off in months. The work had been exhausting and the last thing any of them wanted was to be stuck here at four in the morning in weather like this.

'Time to get to work,' Camus said.

The job they were undertaking was supposed to have been completed during daylight hours – it was safer that way – but they'd attracted the suspicions of the Romanian police once too often since they'd arrived in the country and they couldn't afford to do it again. That meant toiling under the cover of darkness to avoid detection. The only problem was that working in the night also meant that it was very likely that some of them were going to be killed. Not that the men knew this. It was something Camus had kept to himself.

He scratched his arm. It had been itching for days.

He glanced at the tattoo – a skull inside a diamond. The Sign of Lazarus. The remnant of youthful folly when he had run wild and joined a gang purely because he thought it'd make him cool and tough. Instead it was what had led him here tonight to this godforsaken place. He regretted ever becoming associated with that loathsome group. The tattoo had begun to leak tiny pinpricks of blood in the last few hours. It meant he was close. It had done the same when they had uncovered Attila the Hun's burial site in Istria, but there they had managed to bribe any snoopers and the uncovering had gone smoothly. This one felt different, as if they were teetering on the edge of a precipice and it was only a matter of time before they toppled over into the abyss.

Spending some of the best years of your life looking for coffins wasn't what he considered a useful way to pass the time. He had tried to get out of it, as he was a weasel by nature, but he had been advised to do as he was ordered. Two others had turned the job down before he was offered it. They were both dead now. Very dead, in fact. Dead enough to have different body parts buried on different continents from what he'd heard.

He climbed onto the back of the four-wheel-drive truck and handed out the shovels. He issued all the men with headlamps so that they could see what they were working on, then instructed two of the stronger ones to remove the most important piece of equipment from the back of the truck – a bulky lamp. A powerful spotlight that produced high-intensity UV light. The men struggled under its weight. Their knees trembled and their feet sank into the marshy ground.

'What we want light for?' Alexander, a huge Russian, asked.

'In case your headlamps fail,' Camus replied, hoping that everyone was too tired to see through the flimsy explanation.

'Why not flashlights as back up?'

Thank you, Alexander, you nosy Muscovite, he thought. He needed a distraction and quickly before the others started asking questions too. He slipped his mobile phone from his pocket and held it above his head.

'I have been talking to my colleague and he has authorised me to pay you double if you get the work done in two hours.'

That should focus their minds. Some of the men grunted, others accepted the news with solemn faces. But the possibility of earning extra money enticed them. They were mercenaries after all. They automatically moved into their pre-arranged positions on a piece of wasteland just beyond the graves and tombs. Each had their own space, a metre radius in which to dig.

'I not heard phone ring,' Alexander said.

What was it with this guy and his questions? Should he try sarcasm or intimidation to shut him up? Intimidation probably wouldn't work. The man was tough. He had callouses the size of bumblebees on his hands. And he probably wouldn't understand sarcasm.

'If Alexander doesn't get to work within the next thirty seconds then none of you gets paid,' Camus said.

The filthy looks from the others were enough to make anyone's blood run cold and Alexander was no exception.

'I work, I work,' he said, giving in.

Camus consulted the map one last time. Even with the headlamp it was hard to see it clearly. The light glared against the laminate covering he used to keep it waterproof. Rivulets of rainwater ran across the surface.

It looked liked they were at the right spot.

'Dig,' he shouted, just as a fork of lightning crackled across the night sky. If that's a sign, it's not a good one, Camus told himself. The combination of the rain and electricity in the air, the lamps and the graveyard setting, put him in mind of the end of the world. That's what it felt like to Jean-Paul Camus. The end of the world.

The men got to work. They eased their shovels into the soft ground, pushing down on the blades with hobnailed boots. Their shovels sliced through the earth as Camus lit the first of the many cigarettes he would smoke while the men laboured.

·◆·

They had been digging for over an hour and the lashing rain had finally ceased when one of the men cried out.

'What is it?' Camus asked excitedly. The man was standing up to his shoulders in the hole he'd dug. Muddy water swirled around his knees. The others stopped what they were doing, watching, their faces set to grim.

'I've hit something,' said the man.

'Could be rock,' someone said.

Or it could be what we're looking for, Camus thought with a mixture of excitement and dread. 'Get him out of there.'

A couple of the men helped the digger climb out. Camus slid down the bank sending chunks of earth splashing down. He plunged his hand into the water. Earth, rock and ... metal.

'Get the buckets and clear this water out,' he roared.

After a couple of minutes the hole was almost water-free. Camus took out a pocket-sized LED torch and shone it on the area that had been cleared away. A tiny piece of faded brass peeped out from the clogged earth. Could this be it? After all the months of searching? He could feel his heart pounding, his blood pressure rising. Stay calm, he told himself. In control. Don't let the men know there's anything amiss.

'Five minute break. Smoke your cigarettes.'

He called over the only two non-smokers, men who hated the idea of poisoning their own lungs, which was slightly ironic for one of them since he was known as Igor the Poisoner, and instructed them to follow him. Camus noticed with annoyance that Alexander the

Nosy was ambling over, an unlit cigarette dangling from his lips.

'Help me get the lamp up and running,' Camus said to Igor.

'What is lamp for?' Alexander asked.

'I already answered that,' Camus snapped.

Alexander really didn't want to let the lamp question go, did he? His face had an eerie glow, bathed as it was in the flickering flame of his lighter, as the first tendrils of smoke rose from the tip of his cigarette. Camus had had enough of the Russian. He nodded at Gillespie and Sweenz, two of the larger and more obedient employees. They nodded back. As signals go it was unsophisticated, but it worked. They each grabbed one of Alexander's arms and, despite his fierce struggles, within a minute he was subdued and his arms were tied behind his back with plastic cable ties.

'Why you do this?' he roared.

'You'll see,' Camus said with a smirk.

Gillespie duct-taped Alexander's mouth to quieten his incessant prattle as Igor the Poisoner and his companion moved a generator onto the tailgate of the truck and cranked it into life. It spat out smoke and droplets of strong-smelling fuel as it rattled around, whirring noisily. Camus plugged the lamp into the generator, but didn't switch it on.

'You know what to do,' he said, when the men had finished their cigarettes. Some of the mercenaries looked at him through narrowed eyes. He knew what they were thinking. They didn't trust him. His cover story had been that he was an archaeologist in search of an ancient skeleton, but he knew that none of them really believed that. He didn't want to think about what might happen if any of them even suspected the truth. He'd have to watch his back. His front as well. This was going to be a tricky night.

Another half-hour's work in cramped conditions and they had uncovered the jewel-encrusted brass coffin. It was muddied and the shine had long since gone from it, but it could be restored to its original lustre. Not that Camus cared.

'How much is it worth?' someone asked.

'Whatever you can get for it. The coffin is yours. I only want the bones inside.'

He could see the glint of greed in the men's eyes. They were calculating what the bones inside the coffin must be worth if he was willing to give away the jewels with hardly a second thought. He knew that some of them were weighing up the pros and cons of killing him and stealing whatever lay within. Would they risk it before it had even been opened? He'd better not give them the chance.

'Bring it up,' he commanded.

They tied lengths of rope around every handle, then hauled it up until it sat on the wet ground.

And what waited within the coffin awoke.

Eleven

It was after midnight when Colm woke up, feeling hungry. The house was silent. Rubbing the sleep from his eyes, he wandered downstairs in his pyjamas. The ones he really hated. It wasn't that he had anything against pyjamas as such; I mean they're just the things you wear in bed. But these were different. How? Well, for one thing they were girl's pyjamas. Silky pink things with little red love hearts dotted all around. His mother said she'd picked them up by mistake when she was in Dunnes. Colm wasn't sure he believed her. Sometimes he got the feeling that she would have preferred it if he was a girl. She said she'd return them to the shop, but she never had and now he was forced to wear them when his other pairs were in the laundry. If anyone ever saw him wearing them he thought that he'd have to emigrate immediately or else face a lifetime of humiliation.

He stumbled into the kitchen and flicked on the light. He wondered if his mother was home from her night out. He hadn't heard her come in. He wasn't exactly scared of being in the house by himself, but he didn't feel good about it either, not since that night in the Red House Hotel. What seemed normal during the day always seemed to take on a more menacing aspect after midnight. The stillness was almost eerie and the moonlight streaming through the kitchen window only added to his unease.

The moment of anxiousness ended when his stomach began to rumble. He took three packets of cereal from the press and poured some from each box into a bowl, then splashed on the milk. Half of it ended up in a pool on the floor. Must mop that up in a minute, he thought, as he began to crunch his way through what he liked to call a Cereal Bomb. The clock on the wall said it was ten to one. Without warning, the memory of his behaviour at the party hit him again and he cringed. He shut his eyes, but it wasn't enough to block out what had happened.

His train of thought was broken when he heard a noise upstairs.

At first he didn't think anything of it. It was probably just a window blowing open in the wind. Except it wasn't a windy night. Then he heard a grunt. Windows didn't grunt. Someone was trying to break into the house. There had been three burglaries in his estate already this year. And now his house was going to be the fourth.

Colm felt the slow crawling sensation he hated. The general who led the bad feeling brigade marched his troops down into the pit of his stomach. Calm down, he told himself. It's probably just your imagination. But he didn't believe that. His father said that bad luck always comes in threes. After the run-in with the wheelie bin and the disaster of the party, he'd already had two. Was this the third? Yep, looks like it, he thought, as whoever was climbing in through the bathroom window landed with a soft thud on the tiled floor.

His mind began to race. He had to get out of here. He put the cereal bowl on the table and had started to move towards the front door when he remembered he was still in his pyjamas. If he ran outside to raise the alarm then all the neighbours would see him and they'd never let him forget it. His life was enough of a joke as it was. On the other hand, if he stayed where he was the burglar might cause him serious injury. Humiliation or hospital? Before he had the chance to decide which he preferred, the decision was made for him. The burglar was coming down the stairs, blocking Colm's route to the front door.

He looked around the kitchen frantically. There was nowhere to hide. He thought about crawling under the table, but that was probably the first place the burglar would look. If it was a burglar. What if it was someone connected to the rat-faced man? Someone looking for revenge. He gulped. Twice. He needed a weapon. Something he could use to defend himself.

He had a choice of a dirty saucepan or the sweeping brush. He grabbed the saucepan. What now? If he pressed himself right up against the wall beside the door, then, when the intruder came into the kitchen, he wouldn't see Colm. Not at first anyway. Colm would have the element of surprise. Then he'd whack the man from behind with the saucepan. He lifted it above his head, getting it into prime whacking position, and took a step towards the door, flinching as he saw movement in the corner of his eye. Then he realised it was his own reflection he had seen.

The patio door! What was wrong with him? He could have escaped that way. But it was too late. The intruder was on the second last stair. Colm could just make out the toe of his trainers. At least that meant it wasn't some kind of supernatural entity. They rarely wore Nike.

He had to get into position. But as he took another step forward his foot slipped on the wet floor. The spilled milk, Colm thought as he flew into the air and landed on his back with a horrible cracking thump. A second later the burglar stepped into the kitchen.

You are without doubt the most useless boy in the history of the world, Colm said to himself as he waited to meet his fate.

Twelve

Inside the coffin that sat upon the muddied earth of the wet and windy Transylvanian graveyard, lay what was once Vlad the Third, Prince of Wallachia. In his heyday he had been known by many as Vlad the Impaler, by others as Dragul, and by those who believed in the supernatural as Dracula. Yes, that Dracula. He had been in the coffin for five hundred and thirty-five years now, yet he was still alive. Barely. There was only a tiny drop of existence left in him. The part of the brain that had once been home to emotions and feelings, no matter how cruel, had long since died and what was left was a creature that wanted nothing more than to feed, even if it didn't know why. Vlad would have smiled if he had lips or anything resembling a mouth. His organs had long since turned to jelly and the blood that flowed from his heart pulsed slowly now, a mere trickle from a chest that had once beat with a fierce passion. What lay in the jewel-encrusted box had long since ceased to resemble any form of human. Despite the aura of magic in his resting place, Vlad had still faded over the centuries.

His forefinger, almost desiccated now, twitched slightly. Life was all around him. He could sense the men. He could be reborn. Vlad had spent far longer in this coffin than he had above the ground and for the first three hundred years, when he still had his faculties, he had been heartily sick of it. Being dead probably wasn't much fun, but it certainly would have been more pleasant than being buried alive. He was supposed to be immortal. That is how it should have been. But he had been tricked by his enemy Basarab Laiotă and now he was stuck here dying ever so slowly.

Over the centuries, while he could still think and feel and remember, he had heard the people in the nearby cemetery – the solemn, thoughtful ones visiting and tending to the graves of their relatives, the idle youth drinking cheap alcohol and telling ghost stories, the lonely, the bored, the rich and poor. So many people. So many different people. Every footstep, every cry of pain or peal of laughter pierced his slowly dying heart. How he had longed to be up there among all that life. Just so he could kill anything that moved.

But he had never been able to escape, and over the centuries, as he had slowly decayed, he had fallen into a trance, kept alive only by the possession of that horrible thing that lay alongside him in his prison. The Lazarus Key. Wretched thing. It had been nothing but a curse to him. Once he had been a cold and callous ruler, a killer, the most feared man within a thousand miles. Now he was nothing. It was at that moment that Vlad the Impaler became aware that he was thinking again. And that his body was growing stronger. His senses were becoming heightened. Was it the men above him? The fresh, living men? They didn't know how good it was to be alive, to taste the fresh air, to eat and laugh. Taking it all for granted.

The key began to glow.

But it wasn't just the presence of the men that was causing the transformation, although it was certainly part of the reason. There had been visitors before and the creature that had been Vlad hadn't returned to life then. He was doing so now because unbeknownst to everyone except his boss – The Ghost – Camus held the second Lazarus Key. It was wrapped in a purple velvet cloth, tucked away in his jacket.

Camus took a few steps backwards until he was beside the spotlight. He unzipped his jacket pocket and took out the key and, being extra careful to ensure it remained safely wrapped in its cloth, enclosed it in his fist. The fingers of his free hand twitched nervously as they hovered over the ON switch. He tried to order his thoughts. He had to be steady and in control. His life depended on it. The other men's lives depended on it too, but he wasn't worried about them. 'Open it,' he shouted.

The men shoved each other, fighting like school-children, eager to be the one to open the coffin. They slid the tempered steel of their shovel blades into the spot where they imagined the seal between the lid and the main body of the coffin should be. They poked and prodded, cleaning out centuries of dirt and stone and dead worms, but they couldn't force the coffin open.

Igor the Poisoner stepped forward.

'Back,' he commanded in his strong, thick accent.

Nobody moved until he produced a small brown bottle of foul-smelling liquid. They gave him a wide berth then. A single drop of one of Igor's potions was reputed to be enough to bring down an angry bear. He uncorked the bottle and emptied a little along the brass edge.

A wisp of smoke escaped as the pungent liquid took seconds to eat through what had taken centuries to build up.

'Is good stuff,' said Igor, grinning toothlessly.

The men took a further step backwards. Even if Igor didn't have evil intentions, none of them wanted to be splashed by something that potent. They allowed him to continue his work in silence until all that kept the coffin closed was a series of padlocks of ancient design.

Alexander watched, still captive. He noticed that the coffin was in remarkably good shape for something that had been buried for so many years. His keen senses were also aware of something else. Something that disturbed him. He knew that he had to get away from there.

Igor slipped a crowbar into one of the brass latches

and levered it until it began to bend. The lock popped open suddenly. The men's eyes widened. Some of them licked their lips in anticipation, even though they had no idea or expectation of what opening the coffin would reveal. Only five locks to go. Igor's grin grew wider as he moved on to the next one. And the next one.

Alexander realised that the grip of the men who were holding him had slackened. They were distracted by the show. He began to cough and splutter. It was enough to attract their attention. Sweenz glanced at him, his headlamp illuminating the prisoner's face which had turned an unhealthy shade of crimson.

'He can't breathe,' he said.

'So what?' said Gillespie, who wasn't a particularly sensitive type. Sensitivity isn't usually a trait associated with ruthless mercenaries.

'He's annoying me. Take the tape off his mouth.'

Gillespie sighed. This was interrupting the show. He'd take it off all right, then he'd give Alexander a couple of swift kicks for daring to have respiratory problems while he was in charge of him. He ripped off the tape as quickly as he could, hoping it would hurt like hell. He forgot to resume his grip on the prisoner.

Alexander coughed one last time, then, still on his knees on the wet grass, he looked up at the man and whispered something inaudible. He had a devilish plan. One that would set him free. A plan so cunning that it would be the model used for every escaping hostage for a thousand years. Gillespie was about to lean over to hear what Alexander was whispering when the scream distracted them.

It wasn't a pleasant girlish scream. It was one of sheer terror. Of someone who had just seen something his mind couldn't comprehend. Of someone who had just experienced the most horrific moment of his life. And this was someone who'd been involved in some supremely nasty events. Sweenz released his grip on Alexander and stepped forward to get a better look at what was happening.

Alexander knew when to take his opportunity. No time to hesitate. No time to look and see why the man was screaming even though every curious bone in his body wanted nothing more than to have a gawp. The devilish plan would have to wait for another time. He took off, his hands still tied behind his back. He stumbled as he reached the crumbling stone wall dividing the cemetery from a darkened forest. He pushed off his left leg and leaped into the air, catching his right foot on the top of the wall. He fell to the ground, rolled over, clambered to his feet.

As he thundered through the thick grass and sticky mud, Alexander promised himself that if Camus survived this night, he would find him and make him pay for his disrespect. He would make him beg for forgiveness and then he would kill him. No one had ever treated him like this before. No one. He had made him feel like a common citizen. Him! The great Alexander. He would track Camus down even if he had to travel to the ends of the earth. He would track him down and destroy him. He swore on the graves of both his wives and three of his dogs. The mercenary reached the edge of the forest and was swallowed up by the darkness.

What he left behind was a scene of devastation.

When Igor had broken the last lock, he'd grunted with delight. All these tough men and he'd been the one to do it. He'd pressed his fingers against the lid and prised it open. A cloud of mist had emerged, hanging in the air above the coffin. Igor had reached in, his hand disappearing from view. His fingers brushed against something. It felt like … a diamond. He knew what they felt like. He'd stolen enough of them in his time. He closed his fist around it and slipped his hand into his pocket.

The cloud dissipated. And then a dark shape had moved towards Igor in a fury, almost swifter than the eye could comprehend.

The creature moved more on instinct than thought. It had enveloped Igor and suddenly he was hidden from view. Before he had a chance to move, to cry out, to even become aware of what was happening to him, he was dead. The scream that Alexander had heard had come from the man standing beside him. And moments later he was dead too.

The thing that had once been Vlad the Impaler fed quickly, drawing the life force from the men in seconds, growing stronger with every moment as panic set in around it. Its dried-up body began to reform. Veins and arteries re-grew. Its heart began to pound. And a voice in its head cried out in exultation:

I am alive.

One of the mercenaries swung his shovel in the direction of the Impaler. It cut through the air, finding space where the creature had been a millisecond before. He heard the hiss in his ear as Vlad the Impaler wrapped its spindly, newly grown flesh around his body. He felt the blood in his veins turn ice cold as the creature dug its long, pointed nails deep into his neck. His lips began to turn blue, his face almost transparent, as the life began to flow from him and into the creature.

'How do we kill it?' one of the men roared. 'Camus? What have you done to us?'

Jean-Paul Camus snapped out of it. He'd been transfixed by the spectacle, watching as Dragul, Dracula, the first vampire went about its work. He'd been idly wondering why the Impaler was using its fingers to feed, not the sharp teeth like he'd seen in films. As the cry of the mercenary snapped him back to reality he berated himself for standing there thinking such a useless thought. Had the creature hypnotised him somehow, to prevent him from doing his job? He'd heard that it had such talents. He realised he was quickly running out of time and needed to press the button. The UV light would destroy the creature and save him from becoming its next victim.

He slammed the palm of his hand on the button and

closed his eyes as he waited for the blinding light.

Nothing happened.

No cries or screams other than those of the men falling to the ground all around him. He pressed the button again and again. Still nothing. He opened his eyes. What had gone wrong? The generator was still running, still bouncing around … that was it. Its movement had caused the cable that connected it to the lamp to fall out. It lay there on the ground. Once he plugged it back in, he'd be OK. He picked it up. The end was wet. He dried it on his shirt, checked it once, twice and thrust it into the socket. When he looked up, the creature was right in front of him, its red, watery eyes filled with animal cunning.

Looks like I've just made the biggest mistake of my life, Camus thought.

The creature hissed and lunged for him.

Camus dodged to his left. Quicker than he'd ever moved in his life. It was still a hundred times slower than was necessary. Vlad the Impaler was upon him. It had been drawing the life from Camus for a full two seconds before Camus was even aware of what was happening. He felt the creature's cruel joy as it began to feed.

Camus's life flashed before his eyes. It was full of regrets.

His fist opened and the Lazarus Key rolled clear of its velvet cloth. The creature stopped gorging. Even though it didn't want to. Some force was drawing it to the key. Something that had a hold on him. It dropped Camus's weakened body to the ground and knelt before the key. The only sounds were the wailing of the wind and, just beneath it, the constant spluttering of the generator.

Camus knew what to do. He felt weaker than he had at any time in his life. If he survived he wasn't sure if he'd recover, but he couldn't let this thing free in the world. He didn't hate life that much. He dragged himself up and crawled on his hands and knees until he reached the lamp. He swivelled it until it was pointing in the direction of Vlad the Impaler.

'Say goodbye, Dracula,' he whispered.

The creature spun around. It didn't know what was happening, but sensed it wasn't good. The man was still alive. Why? It had become distracted somehow. As Camus pressed the button the creature flew at him, ready to cause him pain. The bulb flashed brightly enough to light up a city. And to tear Vlad the Impaler into a thousand pieces. Five hundred and thirty-five years lying in a coffin for two minutes of killing, the creature thought as it exploded. It wasn't worth the wait.

•◆•

It was several hours before Camus had the strength to gather up the two keys and drive away, leaving his fallen employees behind without a second thought. Even though he was weaker, more frail than he could ever have imagined, he would complete his task. His hands were dry and flaky, but he hadn't time to think about that. He would fly to Ireland and deliver the keys to his master just as he'd been told to do.

It was only when he left the dirt roads behind him and reached the motorway that he glanced into the truck's rear-view mirror and saw the face of an eighty-year-old man looking back at him.

Thirteen

'What are you doing lying on the floor and why are you wearing those stupid pyjamas, ya big eejit?' The Brute asked.

The Brute was Michael James McGrath, Colm's first cousin. They didn't like each other. Not even a little bit. The Brute didn't like his cousin because he thought he was wimpy, needy, whiny and boring. Colm didn't like The Brute because he thought he was a bullying thug who had more t-shirts than brain cells.

The Brute had once spent a fortnight with Colm and his parents and for Colm it had been the worst two weeks of his life. Their last night together had been the one they had spent at the Red House Hotel. After that they'd both developed a small bit of respect for each other. But they still didn't like each other. Like didn't come into it at all.

Colm had seen Michael only once since then, when they'd both attended a dull family get-together. The Brute had insulted Aunt Maggie's new baby boy by telling everyone he reminded him of Gollum from *The Lord of the Rings*. Their fiery young cousin Isobel had stood up for Aunt Maggie and kicked The Brute in the shins. It had cheered everyone up.

Colm would have almost preferred if it had been a burglar, or even just your ordinary common-or-garden assassin, who had arrived at his house in the dead of night. It would have been much less embarrassing than The Brute seeing him like this. Of all the people he didn't want to find him lying on the kitchen floor in a pool of milk while dressed in a pair of girl's silk pyjamas dotted with pink love hearts, The Brute was number one, two and three on the list.

'I fell,' Colm replied after what was possibly the longest ever pause between a question being asked and answered.

'That still doesn't explain the pyjamas,' The Brute

smirked.

Colm picked himself up off the ground and ignored the comment. 'What were you doing climbing through the window like that? I thought you were a burglar. You nearly gave me a heart attack.'

'Boo hoo. You're still alive, aren't ya, so stop whinge-ing. Anyway, I rang the doorbell seventeen times. It was rude of you not to answer.'

'I didn't hear it, I was asleep.'

'You were too scared to answer it, is what you mean,' The Brute said. He opened the fridge door. 'I'm starving. What have you got to eat?'

'You still shouldn't have climbed through the window,' Colm said.

'We're family. That means we can do whatever we want.'

'No, it doesn't. Family means we have to look out for each other.'

'Where did you learn that? From Barney the Dinosaur? Look out for this,' The Brute said, flinging a natural yoghurt at Colm.

It caught him right on the nose, the carton bursting open on impact and covering Colm's face with its healthy gloopiness.

'Ow.'

'I told you to look out. It's not my fault if you have the reflexes of a drunken goat.'

'What are you doing here anyway?' Colm asked.

'None of your business. Where's Auntie Mary?'

'That's none of *your* business,' Colm replied, cleaning his face with a tea towel. 'You're such a jerk. You promised you wouldn't hurt me again.'

'Doesn't sound like something I'd say,' The Brute replied. 'Anyway, who gets injured by yoghurt? There must be some decent food in the house. Where do you keep the crisps?'

'We don't have any. And you *did* promise me you wouldn't be violent any more. The night you found the Lazarus ...'

The Brute's face was suddenly ablaze with fury.

'Don't ever mention that night,' he roared. 'Ever.'

'OK, OK. Relax.'

'DON'T TELL ME TO RELAX. I AM PERFECTLY CALM. DON'T I LOOK CALM TO YOU?'

'Well, your eyes are popping out, your face is bright red, and you've just spit all over your own chin. So to answer your question, no, you don't look calm,' Colm said.

The Brute burst into laughter. 'I'd forgotten what an annoying mammy's boy you are.'

Colm was taken aback by his cousin's sudden transition from anger to what appeared to be good humour, but he held his ground. 'You've also forgotten you promised ...'

'I haven't forgotten. I have an excellent memory. You told me not to hit you. You were acting all tough and after ... y'know, that night ... I took pity on you.'

'I'm telling you now: don't ever hit me again.'

'Oooh, I'm scared.'

'I've been learning karate,' Colm said.

'I know. I heard you busted some poor guy's nose. Snot a good day for you.' The Brute laughed at his own joke.

'It was an accid—'

'Sounds cool to me. OK, you get me something to eat, I promise not to hit you again,' The Brute said.

'Are you crossing your fingers behind your back?'

The Brute held up his hands. 'Nope. Straightforward promise.'

Colm climbed onto the kitchen counter and reached up to the top of the cupboard where his mother kept her 'only for special visitors' biscuits hidden. He threw a packet down to The Brute, who ripped the foil open and stuffed three of the cookies into his mouth.

'Good lad,' he spluttered.

'So no hitting. No more daily digs.'

'Definitely no hitting,' The Brute said. I never mentioned kicks, throws or trips, he thought, as Colm hopped down.

'Are you going to tell me what you're doing here?' Colm asked.

'Sure. Change out of those pyjamas first. I can't talk to you when you're dressed like that.'

·◆·

'Now I can look at you without laughing,' The Brute said, after Colm had changed into a shirt and jeans. Then he started laughing. 'No, seems like I can't. It's your stupid face. Cracks me up every time.'

Colm began to wonder if getting a dig in the arm would be better than The Brute's feeble attempts at humour.

'Can you stop stalling and explain why you came here in the middle of the night?'

'Might be past your bedtime, Geekmeister General, but it's not the middle of the night.'

Colm peered over his glasses.

'Right, right, I'll explain,' The Brute said, taking a sip of the coffee he'd made in Colm's absence. He'd recently begun drinking coffee because he thought it made him seem cool and sophisticated. He also thought that it would make girls like him. He didn't realise that changing his personality would have been a better road to travel.

'I've run away from home,' he said. 'Seanie was doing me head in. He was always telling me what to do and all that, but since he married me ma, it's got way worse. It's been hell.'

'Really?' Colm asked. That was serious. Poor Mich– … he caught himself. He'd started to feel sorry for his cousin. This had been a road *he'd* travelled before and it always ended in either an insult or a punch. He wasn't going to let that happen this time.

'Can you explain the whole "hell" thing?'

'Yeah, I have to clean my room and do the ironing and stuff. That's Mammy's work.'

'Mammy?'

'I mean me ma,' The Brute said, reddening at his mistake.

'But I have to do stuff like that all the time,' Colm said.

'That's 'cos you're a girl.'

'No, it means … forget it. It still doesn't seem like a reason to run away from home though. Shouldn't you give them a call? Let them know where you are.'

'I left them a note. Told them where I was going. They know where to find me if they want to talk. Where are your folks? Thought they'd be downstairs by now, all concerned and stuff,' The Brute said.

'Dad's working. Ma's out.'

'And they left you here on your own?'

'Something like that.'

'Wow, things have changed around here,' The Brute said. 'So when's your ma coming home? I presume she'll want to give out to me for running away.'

'Of course she will, she's …'

'Not interested any more. You've bored me so much I'm surprised I haven't fallen asleep already. I'm going to watch TV.'

Colm followed him into the living room. The Brute threw himself onto the couch and pressed a button on the remote. The television came to life. One of the shopping channels.

'Rubbish,' The Brute said, changing channels. A sitcom.

'Seen it,' he continued.

He flicked from station to station, a comment of disapproval for each one. It wrecked Colm's head. There was nothing worse than someone with a short attention span being in charge of the remote. Now The Brute had found a late-night horror movie. A bunch of zombies surrounding a shopping mall. Pale blue faces. Slow, jerky movements. Pawing at the doors trying to break through to the regular humans locked inside.

Finally, thought Colm, something The Brute would enjoy. His cousin was always banging on about how much he loved scary films. The more blood and guts the better. Colm couldn't stand them. Yet another difference between them. He wondered how two sisters who had loads in common could have two sons who were polar opposites. Life was strange.

He wondered if he should sneak out and phone his

mother and his aunt while Brutie Boy watched the film. It seemed a bit of a tell-tale thing to do, but at the same time he knew his aunt would be frantic with worry about her little boy – although calling him a little boy was a bit of a joke. There were some WWE wrestlers with less muscle mass than his cousin. He'd grown taller and stronger since the last time he'd seen him. His little moustache had grown less wispy as well. And Colm also noticed, now that he came to think about it, that his skin was sort of orange. Was The Brute actually wearing fake tan? He'd never understand him. Never. Colm still hadn't decided whether or not to make the call when he noticed that the television had been switched off.

'Why aren't you watching the film? I thought you liked horrors,' he said.

'Didn't feel like watching it,' his cousin replied, but he didn't meet Colm's eyes when he said it.

Then it hit Colm. There were zombies in the movie. The creature that had come after them the night of the Lazarus Key was like a zombie. Normally, he wouldn't have said anything, but he'd made a habit of saying things he shouldn't today, so he said it anyway.

'Is it because there's zombies in it and it reminds you of ...'

The Brute didn't allow him to finish the sentence.

'I TOLD YOU NOT TO MENTION THAT NIGHT. HOW THICK ARE YOU?' he roared.

Colm didn't reply, letting the question of his intelligence remain unresolved. After a moment's silence, The Brute spoke again.

'The creature that night. It wasn't a zombie,' he said.

'Yeah, what was it so?'

'Dunno, but it wasn't a zombie.'

'Zombies are people who die and come back to life. Hugh DeLancey-O'Brien died, was buried and came back to life.'

'Yeah, but zombies also try and eat people. They eat their brains and stuff. It's where they get their nutrition. Must be a lot of protein in brains, I guess. That thing just wanted to take our life force and make itself young or live forever or something. Remember the way the rat-faced guy shrivelled up when the DeLancey creature wrapped itself around him. It didn't start chewing on his arms or face or anything,' The Brute said.

'Good point. And now that I think of it, I don't think

zombies are supposed to be bothered by the light,' Colm said. 'Remember the way the sunlight freaked it out?'

'Vampires can't stand the light.'

'But they suck blood, so we're back to the whole eating thing again,' Colm said. 'Maybe it was some sort of hybrid.'

'What do you mean?' The Brute asked.

'Like the way a liger is a cross between a tiger and a lion. Maybe this was a cross between a vampire and a zombie.'

'That makes the creature a vambie.'

'Or a zompire. Or, like, if it was lying there unmoving for a hundred years it could have been a mummy,' Colm said.

'True. What could we call it then?'

'A vamumzompire?'

'Weak dude, very weak,' The Brute smiled.

The smile disappeared faster than it had arrived.

'Listen,' he continued. 'I didn't ring the bell earlier.'

'No problem,' Colm said. Climbing through the window wasn't really an unreasonable thing to do when you were Michael James McGrath.

'There's a reason I'm telling you this. I snuck in

because … well, because there's something weird happening.'

Of all the people The Brute could have spoken to, Colm was one of the few who could possibly understand what he'd gone through. That sucked. Lauryn was another; he'd have much preferred to talk to her, but she was in America and hadn't answered her phone, even though The Brute had rung her about forty times. He hopped off the couch and began to pace up and down.

'When I left home today, I thumbed a lift to Killarney, then I got the train to Dublin,' he said. 'I should have been here hours ago. I mean I got the right bus and all. The 16a. But I didn't realise they went in two directions, so I ended up in Rathfarnham. Had to get another one back to the city centre. Of course by then the buses had finished for the night and I hadn't enough money for a taxi, so I had to walk here.'

Getting lost was also a typical Brute thing to do.

'I went through all that just to get here. That's a lot to do, right? You wouldn't do that just 'cos you were bored, would ya? You'd have to be serious to do something like that.'

Colm nodded. 'But I still don't underst—'

'Ma and Seanie went out for a meal the night before last. I was at home texting a couple of my girlfriends and I fell asleep on the couch. Didn't wake up until the next morning. It was only then I noticed that they hadn't come home. The bed hadn't been slept in or anything.'

Colm had to admit that that didn't sound good. 'Did you try their mobiles?'

'No, I never thought of that. I just decided to take a trip to Dublin to ask you if you'd seen them,' The Brute replied. 'Course I tried them. Loads of times. And you know what my ma is like. Same as yours. She'd answer her phone even if she was at a funeral.'

'That's true.'

'It gets worse. When I got to your estate, which is a very confusing place, by the way, someone began to follow me. Someone dressed in black. They were big and scary.'

Uh-oh, Colm thought. This is getting worse by the second. He knew he'd heard something earlier. 'Do you know why they were following you?'

'No, so I stopped them and asked.'

'You didn't, did you?' Colm was astonished.

The Brute rolled his eyes. 'Of course I didn't. Don't you know sarcasm when you hear it? I ran. I'm fast, y'know. Fastest in the school. I can outsprint the sixth years. Anyway, I doubled back and ran around the estate, then hopped over your back wall, climbed onto the top of your bins and pulled myself onto the kitchen roof. Then I dragged myself through the bathroom window. I thought if I rang the doorbell whoever was following me might come here and I didn't want to put Auntie Mary in any danger.'

Colm was surprised by his cousin's thoughtfulness. He was usually a 'thinking of number one' kind of fella.

'You think someone's kidnapped your mam and Seanie, don't you?'

'Yep. And I think they're coming for us,' said The Brute.

Fourteen

Colm needed to keep a clear head if he was going to get to the bottom of this. Panic was never a friend in times of crisis. He rang his mother's mobile. No answer. He tried his dad's. Straight to voicemail. That wasn't so bad. He was busy at work so he'd probably switched it off. But his mam should have answered. The Brute was right about that. She always answered her phone.

He went into the kitchen and found his cousin munching his way through another packet of chocolate biscuits he'd managed to liberate from their cupboardly prison. He'd obviously been pacing again because there was a trail of crumbs on the kitchen floor large enough for Hansel and Gretel to follow.

'I eat when I'm worried about something,' he said. 'So, what do we do now?'

'We ring the gardaí,' Colm said.

'And tell them what? That nearly two years ago we were attacked by a vicious zombie ...'

'Vamumzompire,' Colm said.

'That's never going to catch on. It takes forever to say it. "Watch out behind you, there's a vamumzom–" You'd be dead meat before I'd finished the sentence. Anyway, stop interrupting. Where was I? Oh yeah, attacked by a vicious ... thing that had been brought back to life by a magical key which was wanted by a man who just happened to be the world's most dangerous criminal, but we destroyed them both and now we think someone's after us probably looking for revenge,' The Brute said.

'No, we won't tell them that because that'd sound stupid. We tell them that your parents have disappeared ...'

'SEANIE'S NOT MY DAD!' The Brute roared. He took a calming breath and said in a more normal tone, 'I have a dad and he's brilliant. OK?'

'OK,' Colm nodded. 'Sorry. We tell them that your mam and *stepfather* have disappeared, we can't get in touch with mine and we're stuck on our own. If they believe us they'll search for them and put us someplace safe. If they don't, then we'll have to look for them ourselves.'

'You're right. That sounds like a better idea. That's why you've got the brains and I've got the looks.'

'The looks of an orangutan,' Colm muttered.

He rang directory enquiries and asked for the number of his local garda station. The operator patched him through.

'It's dialling now,' Colm said.

The Brute gave him the thumbs-up, somehow managing to make the gesture appear threatening.

'Hello, Whitehall Garda Station,' said a female voice.

The doorbell rang.

'It'll be your mam. I'll get it,' The Brute said and legged it.

'No,' Colm shouted after him. 'My mam has a key. She never forgets it.'

'That's good to know. Thanks for the information, young man,' said the garda on the other end of the line.

The Brute returned and he wasn't alone. 'I think you'd better hang up the phone,' he said.

Three men followed him into the kitchen. Although Colm didn't know it yet, they were the same three who had kidnapped Kate Finkle earlier that day.

'Hang up and don't even think about asking your phone friend for help if you know what's good for you,' the wiry man scowled. He winced as he said it, still troubled by the cracked ribs Kate had given him. He gave a curt nod and Uggo grabbed The Brute and threw him against the wall. The Brute suppressed a yelp of pain.

'I'll call back later,' Colm said into the phone.

'Can't wait,' said the garda as she hung up.

The Brute got to his feet a little shakily.

'What are you doing here? What do you want?' Colm asked, his thoughts whirling around at a million miles an hour.

'You don't ask the questions, I do,' the wiry man replied.

'Don't even think about hurting him,' Colm said. It made him sound far braver than he actually felt at that moment. If they did start beating up his cousin he had no idea what he would do. When it came to fighting Colm was more likely to injure himself than anyone else.

'Hurt him? I hadn't planned on that, but maybe I should,' grinned the wiry man.

'That's it, Colm. Give 'em ideas,' The Brute said.

'If you lay one finger on him ...' Colm began in a shaky voice.

'Oh, I won't be doing any of the dirty work. My two employees will take care of that side of things. They'll do whatever I tell them to do,' said the wiry man.

Pretty Boy grunted. It was a grunt that signified 'no', rather than the slightly deeper one that would have indicated 'yes'.

'Definitely not,' Uggo agreed.

'But I'm in charge,' wailed the wiry man. As soon as he'd said it he realised that being whiny didn't make him sound like he was in charge. It just made him sound weak.

'Let's sort this out like men,' The Brute said. 'Three against two just isn't right though, is it? You look like men of honour. I'll take one of you on. Muscle against muscle. Beauty versus The Beast. *Mano a mano*. I win, you apologise and leave.'

'What if we win?' Uggo asked.

'Then you do what you have to do.'

Well, that's about the stupidest idea I've ever heard, Colm thought.

·◆·

Ten minutes earlier Cedric Murphy had been sitting behind the wheel of his car watching the men he'd followed as they in turn had watched a house. Of course it wasn't actually his car. They'd have recognised that in an instant. He'd tried to rent one with his Visa card but the transaction hadn't gone through. He was well over his limit. Luckily, he had a contact in Shannon airport that he'd used before. The man was a big fan of detectives. He thought their lives were hugely exciting compared to his, which was true, and he'd arranged for Cedric to collect this car without paying for it.

'I'll be sacked if my boss finds out I've given you a loaner, so promise me you won't get a scratch on it,' Mark had said.

'I promise,' Cedric replied. 'I'll only be tailing a couple of suspects. I won't be going near them tonight.'

'OK. But not a scratch. And bring it to my office within forty-eight hours. I'm putting it down as a two-day rental with a drop-off in Shannon, so it has to be on time. I can't emphasise that enough. I'm doing you a big favour, so, you know, next time you're going on a stakeout anywhere near Limerick you've got to let me go along.'

'You'll be top of my list, Mark. I can't think of anything I'd rather do with my time than sit in a car and tell you all about my life as a detective.'

'Really? That's very nice of you. Thanks!'

Cedric sighed. Mark didn't get it. Kate Finkle would have understood that he was being sarcastic. In fact, she'd have just said something deeply hurtful in reply. It was at times like this that he really missed her. He had been putting off making the call to tell her he was going to have to let her go from her job. Now that he thought of it though, it was strange that she hadn't rung him. She usually did, just for the company, or to nag him about something he had or hadn't done. Mainly the nagging. Was she OK? Maybe he should swing by her apartment and …

'So you'll have the car at my office by 7 a.m. on the 1st,' Mark had said, interrupting Cedric's train of thought.

'I can guarantee it,' Cedric lied.

When he'd collected the car – a nice, comfortable,

but not particularly speedy, black saloon – he'd checked the tracking device and followed it until it led him to this place. He had stopped just down the road from the two-bedroom townhouse in a boring suburb the men were parked outside. Cedric couldn't imagine what sort of business they had here. Some sort of stakeout probably. It seemed like a nice enough place to live, he thought. No litter on the ground. Tasteful shrubbery. Hanging baskets. Lawns cut in a uniform fashion. Must have a good residents' association. He couldn't think of anything duller than growing up and becoming a member of a residents' association. One minute you're ten years old and dreaming of playing professional football or becoming a rockstar or an astronaut, the next you're a member of the local residents' association and genuinely worrying about things like the fact that the neighbour hasn't cut their lawn in three weeks and the place looks a bit raggedy. I hope I'm dead before I start thinking like that, he thought.

The car doors opened and three men got out. Hey-ho, here we go, Cedric said to himself. Now we'll see what you're up to. One of the men was smaller and skinnier than the others and seemed to be talking at a mile a minute. The other two were big bruisers. Professionals by the looks of things. Dangerous. He recognised one of them, the less handsome of the two, as the man who had thrown him down the stairs. They followed the wiry man, who was still talking. The two goons exchanged glances and one of them made a gun sign with his thumb and forefinger aiming it at the back of the skinny guy's head. They both laughed at that.

They reached the door and rang the bell. The two men snapped into pro mode. They drew themselves up to their full height and put on their game faces, determined to intimidate whoever was in the house. Cedric wondered why they were taking this approach – no one going around the back to make sure someone wasn't going to make a run for it. That meant one thing. Whoever they were calling on wasn't expecting trouble. Well, you're just about to get it, you poor sucker, Cedric said to himself.

The door swung open. The guy who answered it was big for his age, but still just a kid. Couldn't be more than fifteen or sixteen. He switched on the porch light just as the men shoved him back inside the house. Cedric caught the merest glimpse of his face.

He's a bit more orange than I remember, but I know him, he thought. He didn't rush in to save the kid from whatever was happening though. Cedric wasn't a big fan of unnecessary heroism. Especially when there was no one around to appreciate it. Where's the residents' association and the nosy neighbours when you need them, he wondered. When he saw that there were no curtains twitching or anybody running over to check what was going on, he grew restless. He could hear Kate's voice in his head: 'Get over there and help that young fella, you big, selfish lump.'

He decided to ignore it. He wasn't going to live a very long life if he listened to his conscience. It only ever got him into trouble. He settled back into his seat and turned on the radio. That would pass the time. No, he wasn't going in. Definitely not.

As he was trying to get comfortable he noticed a girl dressed in black racing across the road. Where had she come from? Had she been hiding there all along? He watched, almost in disbelief, as she ran along the narrow drive that led to the house, then leaped over the wrought-iron gate that separated the front garden from the back, before dropping out of sight on the far side.

'This just got really interesting,' Cedric said to himself.

Was the girl following the men too? Or was she there to help them? Over the next few minutes his conscience reared its ugly head again. A kid? A girl? Against those guys? He sighed. Sometimes he really, really hated his life. Really. Thanks, Kate, he said to himself as he got out of the car. Thanks for five years of service and the way you drip-fed me honesty and morals when they are the very last things a private detective needs.

He was right. But one thing a private detective definitely does need is to be observant and if Cedric had been more observant at that moment he might have noticed the bounty hunter who had also been watching what had unfolded.

'Busy here tonight,' McGrue said to himself.

Fifteen

Cedric Murphy arrived in the kitchen of Colm's house and was struck by two thoughts:

1.   Why on earth would supposedly professional muscle men go into a house at three in the morning and forget to close the front door behind them?

2.   How odd it was to enter a stranger's kitchen and find a teenage boy doing an over-elaborate stretching routine in preparation for a fight with a thug.

Cedric's entrance wasn't as discreet as he'd planned. It was impossible to creep into a house as quietly as a well-trained ninja when you were seven stone heavier than your ideal weight. Especially when you knocked over a vase sitting on the hall table and sent it crashing to the ground. Pretty Boy spun around and gasped as the private detective tried his best to look cool, calm and collected.

'What you doing here?' he asked.

'Thought I'd pop round for a coffee,' Cedric replied. If you thought private detectives were always ready with a witty reply, now you know the truth.

The Brute stopped doing his warm-up exercises while Colm stared at the newcomer open-mouthed. It was *him*. The guy who'd turned up in the middle of the night at the Red House Hotel. Cedric winked at them. It was a wink that told them to keep their mouths shut.

'Who's this balooba?' Uggo snarled.

'Your friend and I go back a long way. We've had some laughs together. Remember? You, me and the stairs. Good times,' Cedric said.

'Yeah,' Pretty Boy chuckled. 'I threw him down stairs. He get hurt. Hurt bad.'

'Careful now, you don't want to use too many big words. Big words cause sore brain.'

'You threw him down the stairs? Him? I'm impressed. He must weigh a ton,' the wiry man said.

'I hope you're not saying I'm fat,' Cedric said. 'I'm very sensitive about my weight.'

'Fat? Man, you're so fat, if they'd dressed you in grey you could have played the boulder in that Indiana Jones movie,' Wiry said.

'Wow. What an intellect. If only it could be used for good rather than evil.'

'You're so fat, they should have just greased you up and used you to plug that BP oil spill,' the wiry man continued, his rudeness growing by the second.

'OK. You've had your fun. Ease off now,' Cedric replied.

'If you jumped in a swimming pool you'd cause a tsunami.'

'Let's see how many offensive jokes you make when I put my fist in your face,' Cedric said.

'That's not going to happen,' said the man with a smirk that made you want to do exactly what Cedric had said. 'Those two have my back,' he said, jerking his thumb over his shoulder in the direction of his companions. 'They'll be on you like a ton of bricks before you can even think about hurting me.'

Cedric looked at the two thugs. The two thugs looked at him. An understanding passed between them.

'Mind if I hit him, just the once?' Cedric asked.

Uggo shrugged. 'Be my guest. You've earned the right to a free one. My brother struggles with his weight and it's not a laughing matter. I hate people who say things like that. It's nasty.'

'Wait, what?' screeched the wiry man. 'You have to stop him. It's your job!'

'Our job's to bring the two kids in, *Boris*. If you happen to get hurt in the struggle, there's nothing we can do about it,' Uggo said.

'But there's no struggle. None. He's just threatening me. That's illegal. And very mean,' said Wiry Boris, his voice rising to such a high frequency that in the back garden a mouse and a bat exchanged concerned glances.

'Hit hard. He's pain in … bum,' Pretty Boy said.

Cedric Murphy snaked out a fist, his hand moving faster than his bulk should have allowed. It connected with the wiry man's nose with a cartilage-smashing crunch. Boris's eyes watered. His knees wobbled. He slumped to the floor like a pile of dirty laundry.

The sudden silence was a welcome relief to everyone.

'*Thank you*,' Uggo said. 'We should have done that ages ago.'

'And as a gesture of gratitude, you're going to head out the door and leave us to get on with our lives?' Cedric queried hopefully.

'What do you think?'

'It was worth a try. So how are we going to do this? Me against you? The three kids versus your buddy?'

'Yeah, we could do it that way,' said Uggo. 'Or … wait a second. You said three kids. There's only two kids here. The little guy with glasses and the orange kid.'

'Orange? I'm not orange. I'm lightly tanned. We had a very good summer y'know,' The Brute said defensively. 'Warmer than expected.'

'Gotta learn to count, big guy,' Cedric said. 'There's three children here.'

Uggo did count. He got to two. It was a struggle. His face was a mask of confusion. What did the detective mean? 'Is this a trick?'

'I mean at the end of July, it was over twenty-three degrees every day for a fortnight. You'd have be allergic to the sun not to be tanned after that,' The Brute rambled on.

'It's not a trick.' Cedric Murphy shook his head then changed direction and nodded towards the patio door. 'May I?'

'Are you trying to escape?' Uggo asked.

'Of course not,' Cedric said.

'Go ahead then.'

Wow. These guys were either so confident in their own ability that they believed he had no chance of getting away or else they were more than a little dim. Considering they'd already allowed him to knock out one third of their gang, Cedric really hoped it was the latter, or else he was about thirty seconds and a couple of kicks away from a lot of physical pain.

'Like I said, three – two boys and a girl,' he said, sliding the door open.

Eeps, Colm thought. That should have been locked. Lucky Mam didn't come home and find it open. But then he remembered that the predicament he was in probably balanced out that stroke of luck.

'What girl?' Uggo said. 'I've counted three times and there's no girl.'

'I think he's talking about me,' said Lauryn, stepping into the kitchen.

Lauryn, the American girl who had helped Colm destroy the Lazarus Key, was now sixteen years old and very beautiful. Her beauty was the main reason The Brute had fallen in love with her when they'd first met. He'd gone completely doolally and even now, well over a year later, the memory of the kiss she'd planted on his cheek was still strong in his mind. In fact, he'd gone seventeen days without washing that particular part of his face afterwards, until his mother threatened she was going to clean it with a brillo pad if he didn't apply some soap to it immediately. He loved Lauryn more than he loved anything or anyone in the world. Even himself.

Now, older people will tell you that love is a complex emotion and that you can't love someone until you really know them. While there is some truth to that, it is also possible that these people are a little bitter at the fact that they're not young any more and can't experience the feeling you get when you see someone and fall head over heels for them. This means they'll often try to convince others that what they're feeling isn't real.

But for over a year, The Brute had thought of little else but Lauryn. He'd begun following the Philadelphia Eagles, an American football team (although he'd never liked the game before he'd met her), just because she was from Philadelphia. He was even sporting an Eagles t-shirt under his v-neck jumper. He'd also started reading a lot of books just because Lauryn read a lot. And he'd composed many, many romantic poems in her honour, poems with titles like 'I love you more than flies love slurry'. Love will do such things to you.

Which is why when she appeared at the door, he was suddenly frozen to the spot. His heart began to pound wildly, his stomach engaged in risky somersaults until he felt nauseous, and he began to sweat like a horse that's just completed the Grand National. Kind of makes you wonder why people write so many songs about love if that's what it feels like.

So when Cedric Murphy took Lauryn's hand, whispered something in her ear, then shouted 'RUN!', Colm sprinted for the patio door and Lauryn turned and took off into the night. But The Brute just stood there with a remarkably silly look on his face. She's here, he thought, my Lauryn is actually here. Except she wasn't any longer. She was running around the house, leaping over the side gate and heading across the street, Colm only metres behind her.

'What are you doing, you eejit?' Cedric shouted. 'Get out of here.'

The Brute snapped out of it. 'Huh?'

And Pretty Boy was on top of him.

Right, that's it, Cedric thought. In future, I'm only going to try to save people who are smart enough to want to be saved. He grabbed Pretty Boy by the shoulders and began to drag him off and that's when Uggo threw his first punch. His huge, meaty paw caught Cedric on the side of the head from the top of his scalp to the bottom of his chin. The detective's brain rattled in his skull with the force of the blow and his teeth clamped down on his tongue. The world around him began to spin. For those of you lucky enough to have never been in a real-life fight, there's only one lesson to be learned – violence hurts. Cedric was groggy and weak, but he still clung grimly to Pretty Boy.

'Move it, kid,' he mumbled as his tongue began to

swell.

The Brute shoved Pretty Boy with the heel of his hand, then swung an elbow. It caught the thug in the mouth, breaking one of his front teeth, but it wasn't enough to make him let go. He still had a fistful of clothes. So The Brute did the only thing he could think of – he wriggled out of the jumper, leaving Pretty Boy holding the garment. He ran for the door, but Uggo wasn't about to let him go so easily. He took a step towards the boy, his arm outstretched, his fingers reaching for The Brute. Before he had a chance to get a grip, Cedric caught him by the ankles and the goon hit the kitchen floor like a toppled redwood.

The Brute was free and he was fast. Lightning fast. He'd caught up to Colm and Lauryn in seconds. Cedric Murphy wasn't as lucky. He too tried to make it to the door, but Pretty Boy and Uggo weren't going to fail a third time.

They didn't.

'You're going to pay for that,' Uggo said.

'Yeah, I kinda thought I might,' Cedric mumbled.

He closed his eyes and waited for the pain to arrive. He didn't have to wait for long.

Sixteen

Jean-Paul Camus hated Ireland from the very first moment he arrived in Dublin airport. He disliked the accent, the way people called him 'bud' when he wasn't their friend, and it really got on his wick that people loved something as disgusting as cheese and onion crisps. Over the following days he also grew to dislike the tardiness of the buses, the Spire on O'Connell Street and the thousands of people who wore tracksuits even when they weren't exercising. Of course, he failed to notice any of the good things about Dublin, but that's because he was in a terrible mood and people in terrible moods always tend to see everything negatively. You couldn't blame him, I suppose. One minute he was thirty-two years old, in his prime, the next he had the face and body of an eighty-year-old. He'd spent almost two years traipsing around desolate parts of Europe and Asia with the most awful companions imaginable and this was his reward. Sometimes life really sucks.

He left his hotel on St Stephen's Green, wandered slowly around the perimeter of the park, which had been closed since 6 p.m., and made his way to Dawson Street. He descended the steep steps that led to a tiny pub. Once inside, he ordered a drink from the taciturn barmaid who just nodded at him as if talking was too much of an effort. She didn't seem to want to make conversation. Neither did the pub's only occupant, a large, middle-aged fellow who sat at the bar. He had huge, gnarled hands, one of which was firmly wrapped around a pint of plain. The barmaid's name was Siobhán. The drinker's name was Paddy, though most people called him Bullkiller. He sort of insisted on it. I'll bet that tells you what kind of person he was.

Camus made his way to the bathroom. He un-buttoned his jacket and removed the velvet pouch which he kept in a clear ziplock bag inside his pocket. He sighed as he caught a glimpse of his hands. It got to him every time. They were white, pasty and veiny and covered with large liver spots. That was nothing compared to his poor ravaged face. Women had once swooned at the sight of him and during his twenties he'd had a succession of gorgeous girlfriends. Never again, all because that wretched Vlad the Impaler had got his claws into him. Now women held doors open so that he could shuffle through, or even worse, gave up their seats on the bus for him. He glanced at the mirror to find a pair of red-rimmed eyes staring back at him. His hair, what little of it was left, had turned snow white, his cheeks were jowly and as for the huge amount of wrinkles ... well, it just wasn't fair. He'd missed out on so much of life. All those good years gone and here he was at the end of his days because of the search for the stupid keys. He wished he'd had the courage to throw them away, but even now, after all that had happened to him, he was still too scared of The Ghost to disobey him. I'm just a cowardly old man, he thought. A cowardly old man who has to pee forty-eight times a day.

The instructions from his boss had been received earlier that day – a handwritten note delivered to the hotel reception giving him the details of where to leave the Lazarus Keys. He didn't know why The Ghost had chosen this place, a pub in the centre of the city, rather than somewhere out of sight, but he was sure he had his reasons. It must be odd to live like he did: on the move constantly, never allowing anyone to know his identity, and for what? Money and some sort of power? It hardly …

Before Camus had the chance to finish the thought, he felt a stabbing pain in his left arm. He suddenly became light-headed. His chest tightened and he fell to the floor. Within thirty seconds the last drop of life had left him and he was dead. Old age and weakened arteries had claimed him. The pouch holding the keys slipped from his lifeless hand.

Back in the bar, Paddy the Bullkiller greedily eyed the tumbler of brandy sitting on the counter. It was the drink Camus had ordered ten minutes earlier. He picked up the glass and threw the contents down his throat.

'You'd better pay for that,' Siobhán said.

'The old fella'll pay,' Paddy replied.

Once upon a time, people like Siobhán wouldn't

have dared to speak to Paddy the Bullkiller in such a sneery manner. He'd been one of the toughest men in Ireland, always ready to answer a question with a closed fist or a steel toe-capped boot. Beating people up had been his hobby. He loved it. It was much more fun than playing pool.

Despite his nickname, he'd never actually killed a bull, although he had once, after getting drunk and breaking into a wildlife park, found himself in a wrestling match with an ostrich. Nobody ever pointed out to him that calling yourself Bullkiller when you hadn't killed a bull was a bit sad. If they had they'd have been spending a lot of time sipping their dinners through a straw.

Things hadn't been the same for the last eighteen months though. Ever since he'd had a run-in with a creepy rat-faced man Paddy's confidence had gone, and once he'd lost his confidence people had lost their fear of him. He'd become a laughing stock. He had to get away and make a fresh start, so he moved from the town where he lived, leaving his job behind, and for the past six months he'd been in Dublin. No one knew him there. Slowly, over time, he'd begun to feel like himself again. He'd drunk a lot and beaten up a fair few young fellas, just to get back into the swing of things. Now all he needed was a bit of luck and he'd be back to his old self.

He lifted a butt cheek and parped loudly, much to Siobhán's disgust.

'Better out than in,' he said with a belch, as if to emphasise the point.

'Better for you maybe, not for me,' Siobhán muttered.

Paddy climbed off his high stool.

'Just going to the toilet,' he said.

'Thanks. I really needed to know that,' she replied, spraying a can of air freshener around the room.

Ah no, Paddy the Bullkiller thought when he arrived in the bathroom and saw Camus's body lying on the floor. It wasn't that he cared that Jean-Paul had died – he was far too selfish for that. All he was worried about was that he'd have to spend hours talking to the gardaí about how he'd found the body. They'd ask lots of boring questions, again and again and again, until his head was spinning. He knew this because he'd had plenty of experience with the gardaí in his home town after all the fights he'd been in. He'd spent so much time with them he knew what football team each one of them supported, their favourite bands and how many sugars they liked in their cups of tea. All he wanted to do now was to go home, have a few beers and watch a kickboxing film on the telly. No chance of that if the gardaí turned up. He'd better get out of there quickly and let Siobhán find the body later. It'd be her problem then, he chuckled to himself.

He was about to leave when he spotted the clear plastic bag lying beside Camus's outstretched hand. Curious, he picked it up and opened it. He removed the velvet pouch and opened that in turn.

'Up ya boyo,' Paddy exclaimed joyfully when he saw the contents.

There were two diamonds in there. Precious diamonds. Small yokes, but he knew plenty of fellas on the wrong side of the law who'd be able to sell them on the black market. Life had taken a good turn again. About time too, he thought.

He held the two diamonds up to the fluorescent tube lighting to get a clearer look. They were glowing. That was a bit odd. Diamonds didn't normally glow, did they? Paddy wasn't sure. He'd never held one in his hand before. And there seemed to be some kind of tiny skull in the middle of them too. Was it a flaw? Nah, it probably only added to their value. As he rolled them around in the palm of his hand, a feeling of contentment settled on him. That was a sign that everything was all right. He'd begun to feel – how to describe it? – happy. Yeah, happy. It had been an awfully long time since Paddy the Bullkiller had felt that emotion.

He popped the keys back in the velvet pouch, put them in his pocket, stepped over the body of the unfortunate Mr Camus and left the pub whistling a happy tune, much to the surprise of the young barmaid.

Seventeen

'Lauryn, it's great to see you again,' The Brute beamed.

It wasn't really the time or place for a friendly chat and Lauryn either didn't hear him or chose to ignore him. Either way the result was the same. Silence. She ran from one parked car to the next, beneath the flickering street lights, frantically pressing a button on the set of car keys she held in her hand.

'Do you know which car is his?' she asked.

'That one,' The Brute said, pointing to a black car whose lights flashed as it clicked open.

He realised, with the tiniest bit of astonishment, that he was talking to Lauryn as if she was a normal person. He hadn't been able to do that before. Back then everything he'd said had been idiotic. Now he was his old cool self again. Go Superdude, he thought.

Colm turned back towards his house. He wasn't sure, but he thought he heard something that sounded very much like a scream. That wasn't good. Poor guy. Curtains began to twitch. The neighbours had heard it too. They were caught halfway between ringing the gardaí and wanting to stay out of it completely.

'We should go back and help him,' he said.

'He gave me his car keys and risked his own safety just so you guys could get out of there. Going back and getting caught would be stupid,' Lauryn said.

'OK,' Colm agreed, although he wasn't entirely convinced. He wasn't a poster boy for bravery, but it didn't sit right with him to leave the man behind. There was no point in hesitating though.

They piled into the car, The Brute and Lauryn in the front, Colm in the back. Lauryn handed the keys to The Brute.

'Let's get out of here,' she cried. Then she noticed the steering wheel in front of her. 'Oh, crud. I'm in the driver's seat. I forgot I was in Ireland.'

'Look,' Colm said.

Pretty Boy was at the front door of the house. He looked a little worse for wear from his encounter with Cedric Murphy and The Brute. His face was a worrying shade of scarlet and when he breathed through his broken front tooth he produced a soft whistling sound. But he was still going.

The three of them ducked as the thug glanced in their direction, scrunching down low on their seats. He didn't spot them.

His eyes searched the estate for any sign of the escapees. His shoulders hunched, his nose sniffed. It looked like he was trying to smell them out, like some kind of predator.

'Stay down,' Colm whispered.

'Thanks. I was going to beep the horn and give him a wave,' The Brute said.

'We should swap seats. Slide over, Michael,' Lauryn said.

'No point doing that unless we're planning to park here for a while,' The Brute replied.

'Huh?'

'I can't drive,' he said.

'What? But you live in the countryside, don'tcha? How else do you get around?'

'I cycle,' The Brute mumbled. 'Or Ma drives me to the shop or to training.'

'Your mom acts as your chauffeur? At your age? That's gotta be embarrassing.'

'We can't drive until we're seventeen here. What else can I do?' he hit back.

'Tough break. In the States it's sixteen.'

'So you can drive?'

'Sure. I've got a car. A beat-up old Dodge Intrepid, but I like it.'

'That's class,' The Brute said. 'Having your own set of wheels, I mean.' His admiration for her had gone up another notch.

'Hey,' Colm interrupted in a furious whisper. 'Keep it down, will you. You're not on a date. We don't want him to hear us.'

A shadow fell over the back of the car.

'Too late,' said Lauryn.

Pretty Boy stood at the back window framed by the full moon. Grinning hideously. The broken tooth made him look even meaner than he normally did, which wasn't good for the increasingly frayed state of Colm's nerves. He reached out and pressed a button, locking the back door.

Click.

'Yeah, that'll stop him,' said The Brute.

The thug began to pound the window with his bare fists. It would have made more sense to try to break through the window of the driver's door, but sense and Pretty Boy were very infrequent companions. He was strong though. The glass began to give way. A spider's web of cracks crept along its surface.

'It'd be nice to get out of here, Lauryn,' Colm squeaked, 'you know, if you don't mind.'

Lauryn sat bolt upright. She jammed the key in the ignition and turned it. The car came to life with a throaty roar.

'I hate to complain, but we've got about ten seconds before he's inside the car with us,' said Colm.

A few more seconds passed during which time Colm came to the conclusion that this might not be the time for politeness.

'Go, go, go,' he squealed in a voice an octave higher than was bearable.

'I can't drive a stick shift,' Lauryn cried.

'A what?'

'She means the gears. Her car doesn't have a gear stick,' The Brute said. He didn't drive, but he had watched a lot of *Top Gear*.

'The Dodge is an automatic,' she said.

Pretty Boy jumped onto the narrow boot. The car sagged with his weight. He began to stomp on the window. Again and again and again.

'Put your foot on the clutch,' The Brute said as calmly as he could. The sound of cracking glass grew louder. 'Quickly,' he said less calmly.

Lauryn looked confused.

'The pedal on the left,' he said.

The window gave way. The entire section of glass collapsed onto Colm in one twisted and tangled piece.

'Brute, put it into first for her,' he shouted, trying to push the glass back out.

'Don't call me Br–'

'Just do it!'

There was a crunch followed by a loud whine as The Brute slipped the gear stick into first. Pretty Boy reached into the back seat, grabbed the panel of glass by the edge and tore it out through the gaping back window, flinging it behind him. It sailed through the air like a frisbee before skidding along the footpath.

'Accelerator. Accelerator,' The Brute said. .

'Which …'

'The gas pedal,' he translated.

Pretty Boy leered at Colm, a malevolent look creasing his features. He reached in through the space that until recently had been occupied by the back windscreen.

Lauryn hit the accelerator.

There was a tremendous screech as the wheels began to spin. Great white plumes of smoke poured out from under the wheel arches. Pretty Boy stared at Colm with a frown of confusion. Colm stared at Pretty Boy with a very similar expression on his face. Both of them were thinking that the car should be moving at speed and that Pretty Boy should be lying on the ground in a pitiful heap by now. Something had gone wrong.

'Take your foot off the clutch,' The Brute shouted.

Lauryn released the pedal and the car lurched forward. The force of the acceleration was enough to send Pretty Boy spinning through the air like a heavyweight boxer doing a gymnastic routine. And just as you'd expect it to, it ended badly. Here we go again, he sighed, as the road came hurtling towards his face.

The car jumped forward in small bursts as Lauryn tried to get to grips with the accelerator and clutch system. It smashed the wing mirrors and scraped the sides of three parked cars on the far side of the road, before she wrenched the steering wheel to the right, denting a further four cars on the near side. The horrendous wailing of metal scraping against metal filled the night air. Finally, she gained control and managed to steer the car to the middle of the road before driving off with the headlights on full beam. Colm looked out through the empty space of the back window.

Pretty Boy was getting to his feet.

He was dusting himself down.

He was running after them.

'He's indestructible,' Colm muttered.

But he wasn't fast enough to catch a moving car. McGrue, hidden as always, was. Or, to be more accurate, the tracking device he fired from the crossbow balanced between his cheek and shoulder was. He gave a small smile of satisfaction as it tore through the air and embedded itself in the rear bumper of the car as Lauryn indicated left, turned right and the trio exited the estate, leaving an average-sized trail of destruction behind them.

Eighteen

Paddy the Bullkiller was in a jubilant mood. On his journey home from the pub he'd picked a fight with three inoffensive teenagers and beaten them all to a pulp. One of them had even cried huge, salty tears which had given Paddy a warm, fuzzy feeling much like the one most people experience on Christmas morning. Now he was halfway through eating the tastiest snack box ever – grease and tomato sauce sliding down his stubbly chin – and within a few minutes he'd be at home for a televisual rendezvous with The Muscles from Brussels, a certain martial arts expert known as Monsieur Jean-Claude Van Damme. In Paddy's world, this was as perfect as life could get.

And to add a dollop of cream to the apple tart of perfection, an hour ago he'd made contact with a man who was going to price the diamonds the very next day. If they were of good enough quality, which he was sure they were, Paddy would be able to sell them to him for a tidy sum. Enough to keep him in frothy beer and snack boxes for a couple of years at least.

If he hadn't been in such good form, Paddy might have been slightly more aware of his surroundings. He might have noticed the man who had been following him for most of the evening. Although, to be fair to Paddy, the man was somewhat of an expert at staying hidden. That was the main reason they called him The Ghost; you never knew he was there unless he wanted you to know it.

It was very unlike the world's most dangerous criminal to get involved in a mundane situation like this, but the bad timing of Camus's death had forced his hand.

He had watched from the roof garden of the building across the road as Camus had entered the pub right on time. He had realised that something had gone wrong with his plan when Paddy had emerged minutes later with an unnatural giddiness to his step. The Ghost had immediately recognised the effects of the Lazarus Keys on the large man. From that moment, the chase was on. He was an expert at tracking people and Paddy left a trail that even the most bumbling of private eyes could have followed. It hadn't taken him long to catch up with the drunken oaf. Bullkiller had something that belonged to him and he was going to get it back. No matter what it took.

Paddy strolled through the paint-peeled gates of the tumbledown apartment complex, flinging the empty snack box carton onto the road. The Ghost stood and watched him for a moment and then began to close the distance between them. Almost gliding silently. Fifty metres became twenty-five and then ten. Paddy was oblivious to it all.

The Ghost sized him up as an opponent – the man was big and strong, there was no doubt about that. He looked like a fighter, but there was something about his swagger that didn't quite ring true. He was trying to act tough, but there was a chink of vulnerability there, something to be exploited. The Ghost was good at exploiting people's weaknesses. He enjoyed it. He allowed the smirk to stay on his face for exactly one point two seconds before filing it away and getting on with the job at hand.

It took Paddy three attempts before he managed to slip the key into the lock of his apartment's front door. He wrenched the door open and barrelled in, kicking it shut behind him.

Except it didn't shut.

He waited for the thud and the click, but there was nothing. Not a peep. Slowly, he turned to find a man with delicate, almost pretty, features framed by the doorway. Staring at him with cold, cold eyes.

'What ... what are you doing there, ya gobdaw? This is my flat ... isn't it?'

Paddy checked the door. The fog of alcohol clouded his certainty. No, it had the right number on it. Two little aluminium numerals. One and seven. That was seventeen in any man's language. Which meant the man was trespassing on his property. Which in turn meant he could beat him up and pretend that the wimpy geezer was burgling his flat.

I was right – this is the best night ever, he thought. He grabbed the man by the collar and dragged him into the apartment, shutting the door with a swift head-butt that left a little dent in the wood. The man didn't resist. Probably terrified of me, Paddy thought. He couldn't blame him for that.

He shoved the man into the centre of the room. But he didn't look as terrified as Paddy had been expecting. In fact, he didn't look worried at all. The man rubbed his hand across his shaved head.

'You broke into my flat. I'm going to introduce you to a world of pain,' Paddy said. He held up his fists, kissed them in turn. 'This left one is Agony and I call the right one Destruction.'

'It's quite clear that you are a moron,' The Ghost said. 'Hand over what you stole from my colleague and I'll allow you to return to your pathetic life.'

'Huh?'

'The diamonds. Give. Them. To. Me.'

'They're my diamonds,' Paddy said. 'Finders keepers, losers weepers.'

This wasn't going quite how Paddy had expected. No fear, no tears, no whiny begging for mercy. All the good stuff that fuelled his ego was missing. He had planned to pretend the man was a thief, but now it looked like he actually was one. How's that for a bad bit of luck? When all this was over he was going to have a good old sulk.

An unexpected voice momentarily distracted The Ghost's attention from Bullkiller.

'What are you waiting for?' asked the rat-faced man. He was leaning against a counter that divided the sitting room from the kitchen.

When the man spoke The Ghost felt darts of pain at the back of his eye sockets. His brother hadn't been there a moment ago, had he? He couldn't remember. The headaches were getting worse.

'Why are you even here?' the rat-faced man continued. 'This isn't you. Creeping around like a thief. You're powerful. Dangerous. And now you skulk around in the shadows. Why would you do that?' His lips parted in an attempt at a smile. 'Unless you're afraid. Is that what it is? Is my big brother afraid?'

'Shut up,' The Ghost said.

'I didn't say nothing,' Paddy said. He was beginning to have his doubts about the stranger in his flat.

The Ghost rubbed his eyes. When he stopped, the rat-faced man was nowhere to be seen.

'There's two ways of doing this,' The Ghost said, regaining his composure. 'Both of them hurt a lot, but one ends with you remaining alive. In severe pain, but still alive. Technically.'

Paddy suddenly felt queasy. The man was tougher than he looked. And there was something creepy about him. Extremely creepy. The absence of any emotion or humanity. A stillness that filled him with dread. He wanted the man out of his flat. Right now. And the only way to do that was to give him the diamonds.

He looked around his rundown apartment. Everything was either worn or torn and it all smelled more than a bit iffy. He was sick of living like this. If he gave the man what he wanted then he wouldn't be able to do up the flat. No white leather sofa. No fifty-two-inch plasma TV. No heated toilet seat. He needed those things. It was a basic human right to have them.

He would have to stand up for himself. You're too nice for your own good, Paddy, he thought. Just get your act together and smash the man into oblivion. How dare he just waltz in and try to steal from you, he thought, entirely forgetting that he had stolen the diamonds himself only hours earlier.

'If it's a fight you're looking for, you've come to the right place,' Paddy snarled. He began to dance around on the balls of his feet, his stomach jiggling furiously.

The Ghost took a step towards him and Paddy swung a left, then a right. The one-two combination he loved so much. He waited for the familiar comforting feeling of knuckle on jaw, but there was no impact. The man didn't even seem to move, but somehow he managed to avoid the punches. And now he was only centimetres from Paddy's face, his cold, dead eyes staring directly into Paddy's.

The Ghost placed a hand on Bullkiller's shoulder. Immediately, Paddy felt all the fight leave him. The man had barely touched him and he felt terrified. More scared than he'd felt in years. Tears welled up in the corners of his eyes. His lips wobbled. It was as if a psychic message had passed between them the moment the man had touched him. Paddy could have sworn he was seeing all the crimes committed by the man. Horrible, terrible crimes. It was like he was watching The Ghost's gruesome home movie in his mind's eye.

'Are you going to give me what I came for?' The Ghost asked.

'I think I just pooped in my pants,' Paddy the Bullkiller said.

'I'll take that as a yes,' The Ghost replied.

Nineteen

By the end of the journey Colm half-expected to find his hair had turned white with the shock. Of course a quick glance in the mirror confirmed it hadn't. That would have been ridiculous. But he was glad they'd stopped driving. His nerves were shattered, yet his bones were intact, so all things considered, it could have been worse. He didn't know if it was just because Lauryn had had such difficulty with the gears or if she was a terrible driver in general, but he knew that as long as he lived he never again wanted to be in a car when she was behind the wheel.

They had driven through Ballymun and onto the M50, changing lanes at breakneck speed. They'd passed vehicles in which the passengers were gripped with absolute panic when Lauryn's car veered wildly in their direction. Car horns had blared. Fists were shaken. Dogs had stuck their heads back inside car windows until they'd passed. Colm had been so glad to get away from the thugs he'd been happy to let Lauryn drive the car. After forty-five minutes of sheer terror, however, he wasn't sure it was the right choice.

They'd made it as far as Blanchardstown, a suburb on the west side of the city, and driven into a half-finished housing estate, the type the earnest men on serious radio programmes liked to call a ghost estate. Most of the houses were unoccupied and some had already begun to fall down. Grass grew in odd places. Rubble, blocks and discarded, rusted pieces of building equipment were piled on the ground at various intervals. There was an air of sadness about the place.

Lauryn had parked the car at the back of one of the houses, although parked was a kind way of describing it. Unlovingly abandoned at a jaunty angle might have been more appropriate. They'd checked the glove compartment and found a rental slip with the name 'Cedric Murphy' on it, and an almost empty bag of M&Ms.

They'd walked out onto the road to make sure the
vehicle was out of sight and unlikely to be noticed by any
passers-by or local busybodies, and when they were as
sure as they could be that the car was well hidden, they
went into the first house they could access. The Brute
had stuck his hand through a broken pane of glass and
unlocked a window. When they were all inside Lauryn
produced a small torch from the pocket of her black
leather jacket and began to examine each one of the
downstairs rooms in turn, even though she wasn't really
sure what she was looking for or expecting to find. The
interior of the house was as unfinished as the outside.
Everything was grey, as if someone had come in and
deliberately drained the place of any colour. The night
air blew through the spaces set aside for plastic vents,
chilling the open room. It was as unlovely as could be.
There was nothing to sit on, so they sat on the hard
floor.

'OK, does anyone have any idea what's happening?
Because this whole thing seems a bit mental to me,'
The Brute said, goose bumps prickling his bare orange
arms.

'It is kinda crazy,' Lauryn agreed. 'Hey, you're

wearing an Eagles t-shirt.'

'What? Oh, this old thing. I'd forgotten I had it on. Yeah, big fan of the Eagles. Huge,' he replied.

'That's a coincidence. I'm from Philly,' she said.

'Really? Cool,' The Brute replied.

Colm knew that Lauryn had mentioned she was from Philadelphia at least three times when they'd met before. She probably knew it too. And she'd probably guessed his cousin had bought the t-shirt in her honour. Was she just toying with The Brute? If she was, then Colm decided to let her get away with it. After what they'd been through and what they still had to face, she was allowed a private moment of fun.

The Brute leaned back, faking a yawn, stretching his arms to show off his bulging biceps.

'You've been working out for the same reasons as me, I guess,' Lauryn said.

'Huh?'

'To be prepared for the next time we encountered a situation like this. Once bitten, twice shy and all that.'

'No,' The Brute said. 'I've been bulking up 'cos the chicks love it.'

'Excuse me – the chicks?'

Uh-oh, Colm thought. He could hear the tension growing in Lauryn's voice.

'Yeah, the chicks. Y'know, the babes. The broads as you might say in America.'

'I hope you're not talking about girls, 'cos that's totally insulting,' Lauryn said.

'No, what I meant was … ahm,' said The Brute, realising his error and reddening up. He'd suddenly remembered why he used to be tongue-tied around this girl. She was as tough as old boots. Just like her grandmother, Mrs McMahon, who, as far as The Brute was concerned, resembled an old boot. He loved Lauryn, but he was also a little bit scared of her and when he was a bit scared he always said the wrong thing. Always.

'Sorry,' he said. Time to change the subject. 'So, how's your grandmother these days? Still the same old battleaxe?'

'She died.'

The Brute's face was now so red that Colm was genuinely worried that he might be on the verge of a stroke.

'I'm sorry to hear that,' Colm said, trying to calm

things down.

'Thanks,' Lauryn replied.

The Brute slapped the palm of his hand against his forehead repeatedly.

'Soooo, you've gone to the gym a bit?' Colm said to change the subject.

'Sure. I started doing all these self-defence classes, weapons training, running five miles a day. Things like that.'

'But no driving practice, huh?'

Lauryn smiled. 'No, Colm.' She pronounced it 'Collom'. He didn't correct her. 'No driving practice. I didn't just do fitness work, though. I got Prof, that's what I call Peter Drake, to design some brain-training programmes for me. You gotta be sharp, right? I mean anyone can get caught out by a zombie or a criminal once, but a second time ... that'd be dumb.'

'Definitely,' Colm said. 'Very dumb.'

'So what kind of training did you do?' she asked.

'Ahm, we really should be talking about what's going on and what we're going to do next,' Colm said, avoiding the question and at the same time wondering why he hadn't done more to get into good physical shape. If he'd been expecting an attack for all this time, then surely it would have made sense. Yet he'd given up after just three karate lessons. He wasn't exactly Navy Seal material.

'You're right. We've got to figure out what's going on. Then we can take some action.'

'Huighhhhhhhhhhh,' said The Brute, suddenly caught in the halfway house between wanting to say something that would impress Lauryn and wanting to say nothing at all for fear of offending her.

'Huh?'

'I think he's wondering what you're doing here,' Colm said.

'Heeuuuuurgggh,' agreed The Brute.

She brushed a strand of blonde hair back from her tanned cheek. 'It started a couple of weeks ago back in Philly. My Dodge was in the shop so my boyfriend drove me home ...'

There was a strange, hacking sound as The Brute almost choked.

'Boyshfriendsh?' he spluttered.

'Yeah, his name is Dan and he's a running back with our high school team,' she said. 'He's not your typical jock though. He's a straight-A student.'

Of course he is, The Brute said to himself. I hate you, Dan.

She continued her story. As she'd sat in the car chatting to Dan, she'd spotted a man she'd never seen before sneaking out from the back of her house. He'd peered around carefully, as if checking that no one was around, so she'd presumed he was a burglar. He hadn't seen them as they were parked farther down the street, and Lauryn was about to get out of the car and confront him when Dan grabbed her arm and told her to stay where she was. He'd guessed the man wasn't alone. Sure enough, ten seconds later two other men emerged, each carrying what appeared to be a heavy weight in a hessian sack. The sacks were wriggling. Lauryn realised that the only things that could be that size and struggling in that way were her mother Marie and the professor.

As she continued talking, The Brute's thoughts drifted off. Colm and The Brute had met Marie briefly. She seemed like a nice woman, which The Brute thought was a good thing since if he ended up marrying Lauryn, which he planned to do once she'd copped on that Dan was a big tool, he'd probably be having Sunday dinners with her mother and it would make life easier if they got along. Of course that was only if they lived in America, but Lauryn would probably want to stay in the land where she grew up and, with him being the man and all, he'd have to do his best to please her. He wondered if he'd like America. It looked good on the telly, but they didn't seem to play much hurling or rugby over there and those were two of his favourite things in life.

'Hey, are you listening to me?' Lauryn snapped. 'I'm telling you something important here.'

The Brute nodded, snapping out of his little daydream. He hadn't heard a thing she'd said in the last minute and he hoped that she wouldn't ask him any questions or else he'd be caught out like he always was in school.

'Sorry,' said Lauryn, noticing his shame-faced expression, 'I'm a bit on edge. That's why I'm ...'

'Cranky?' Colm volunteered.

'Cranky. Yeah, that's a good word for it,' Lauryn said.

'So your mother and Professor Drake were kidnapped, but you managed to avoid capture thanks to your boyfriend, Dan,' Colm said, recapping for The Brute's benefit. 'Then you tried to follow the kidnappers, but you lost them. You didn't know what to do, so you hid for a few days before sneaking back into your house. You didn't even answer any of Dan's calls 'cos you didn't want to drag him into this mess.'

'Do you recap every time someone tells a story?' Lauryn asked. She kept her tone pleasant, but was thinking: I've teamed up with two imbeciles. She tried to remember if they'd been like this when they'd met before. From what she could recall, the guy who was in love with her hadn't changed that much, except for his cool new haircut and fake tan, and the weird way he kept trying to show off his muscles. Her impression was that Colm had seemed smarter last time, although when she really thought about it, he'd been easily fooled at the start, yet had figured out most of what was going on in the end. Plus it had been him who had come up with the clever way to destroy the Lazarus Key. Maybe she was underestimating him.

'Yeah, I hid out in an abandoned building like this one. It was a horrible place and I was kinda scared 'cos there was a lot of gang activity in the area, but I couldn't risk goin' back to the house in case those guys came back, so I waited a few days before returning. I knew I had to stay free if I was going to be able to help Mom and the Prof. To do that I had to figure out why they'd been taken and who took them. I had plenty of time to come up with an answer when I was sitting in that house day after day,' she said.

'And the answer you came up with was The Ghost,' Colm said.

'Yup,' Lauryn said, thinking that she had underestimated him after all.

'Who?' The Brute asked.

'The little rat-faced man, the one who wanted the key and took us into the woods to meet that zombie … thing,' Colm said. There was no time to explain the whole vamumzompire saga to Lauryn. 'We all thought that he was The Ghost and that he'd been killed by the creature. But I've been thinking. What if he wasn't The Ghost?'

'I agree with you. That's what I think too. And I also think the real Ghost is behind all of this. Who else in this world would have something against the three of us? It's not like we hang out together. We don't even live in the same country. No, this has to be something to do with that night. He took my mom and the Prof. If he was coming after my family, then he'd be going after yours. I decided I needed to be here in Ireland. That was where everyone else involved in the situation that night was. I guessed that's where my mom and the Prof would be taken too. I went back home and got the emergency pack the Prof and Mom had prepared for a situation like this – money, fake ID, stuff like that – then I caught a plane to Dublin. I've been hanging out near your house for the last two days. Freezin' my butt off. I wanted to talk to you, but I thought it'd be better to observe from a distance, see if anything strange was happening. For forty hours there was nothing interesting, other than you coming home stinking up the place real bad. But then I saw Mikey appear and run around in circles for a while, before he launched himself through your restroom window.'

So I didn't outrun the dark figure after all, The Brute thought glumly. Of course, if I'd known it was Lauryn who was following me, I wouldn't have taken off in the first place.

'He looked like he was on the run, like he was

escaping from something, so I hung back, thinking that whoever was after him would show up sooner rather than later. An hour later I saw those three guys going into the house.'

The Brute was impressed. Hugely impressed. Lauryn had managed to evade capture, and survived on the mean streets of Philadelphia and the slightly less mean streets of Colm's housing estate. Not only that, but she'd caught a flight by herself, using a false passport. She was like a super spy. If he hadn't been in love with her before, he'd have fallen for her that very moment. He wondered if he should kick Colm out of the house and tell her how he felt about her. Or maybe he should compose another poem first, praising her beauty and stuff. Chicks loved poems, didn't they? He wasn't sure. Girls were hard to understand, especially when you never spent any time talking to them.

'Wow, you must be wrecked,' Colm said to Lauryn.

'Yeah, I've hardly slept and when I did catch some z's it was on rock-hard ground beneath some shrubbery. Not the most comfortable bed ever created, but when you're tired you'll sleep anywhere. That doesn't matter now. We've got to figure out where this guy has taken

Mom and the Prof.'

'Michael's mam and stepfather have gone missing too. And I can't get in touch with my own parents,' Colm said.

'It's worse than I thought then. We need to plan our next move carefully.'

'I hope you have some ideas,' Colm said.

'No. I don't. Not yet. But we'll come up with something. We're young. We're smart.'

Colm stared at her with a blank face, while The Brute, who was still daydreaming about how he would share his feelings with Lauryn, was looking particularly dopey in the torchlight.

Lauryn revised her opinion. 'Well, we're young anyway,' she said. 'I think the first thing we need to do is figure out where they're keeping your parents. Of course all my cool slayer-type emergency stuff is hidden back near Colm's place. I left it there when I followed the thuggy triplets into your house. Guess I didn't think that through. Anyway, sitting around here is only going to drive me crazy. I hate staying still. We need a lead. A clue. Or just somebody whose butt I can kick.'

The Brute, who had dragged himself back to reality,

slowly raised his hand in the air. It hadn't been easy to work up the courage to say something; after all, every time he did it seemed to upset Lauryn and he didn't want to do that again. Not if he could help it. He cleared his throat.

'Ahm, can I … ahm …'

'We're not in school, Mikey. You don't need to ask permission.'

'I just, y'know, want to make this all clear in my head,' The Brute said. 'We think this Ghost fella hired the rat-faced man to get the Lazarus Key which was buried in the woods near the hotel?'

'Yeah,' Lauryn said.

'And we stopped Ratters and destroyed the key?'

'So far, so good.'

'And now we think The Ghost is getting his revenge on us for stopping his plans?'

Colm and Lauryn both nodded.

'Right,' he said. 'I might have a lead. I think,' he continued, waving his mobile phone in their direction.

The others looked at him expectantly.

'That guy who turned up at the house, the same guy who was at the hotel that night. Remember we saw the name on the car-rental form – Cedric Murphy. Well, I just Googled him and it turns out he's a private detective. The woman who was with him the last time – at the hotel I mean – her name is Kate Finkle.'

They seemed surprised. Or was it more than that? Was it respect in their eyes? It was hard to tell; he didn't know what respect looked like.

'That's great work–' Lauryn began.

The Brute cut her off, his confidence growing by the millisecond as his thumbs worked furiously on the mobile's keypad. 'I've just found Kate's address. I think we should pay her a visit.'

'Definitely,' Lauryn said. She jumped to her feet, a spring in her step, even though she was exhausted. 'Let's go, guys.'

'Are we driving again?' Colm asked.

'How far away is this Finkle woman's home?'

'About ten miles,' The Brute said.

'Then we're driving,' Lauryn said.

Colm's heart sank. He had hoped he wouldn't have to face imminent death again for some time, but thinking about Lauryn's dangerous driving raised an important question.

'One thing: why is The Ghost going to all this trouble? He's this all-powerful criminal. Wouldn't it have been easier for him just to have us killed?'

'True,' Lauryn said, 'but maybe he has something worse planned.'

'Worse? What could be worse than death?'

'I don't know, but I've got a feeling that we're going to find out,' she replied.

'You're absolutely right,' said a voice through the open window.

Twenty

Cedric awoke in the dark with the smell of damp in his nostrils and severe cramp in his calves. He tried stretching his legs in an attempt to ease out the pain, but his way was blocked by something solid and immovable. He waited a few moments, letting his eyes adjust to the blackness and his nose to the musty odour. Where was he? The last thing he could remember was Pretty Boy rushing towards him, a toaster in one hand, a kettle in the other, his face twisted in rage. No need to speculate as to who had won that particular battle. He'd been so stupid. He'd sacrificed himself to save some kids. Again.

What was wrong with him? 'I'm an idiot,' he said aloud.

'Cedric?' said a woman's voice.

'Mum?'

'No, you self-absorbed gorilla. It's me. Kate.'

'Where are you?'

'I'm right beside you, Mr I Detect Things for a Living. Here, put out your hand.'

Cedric reached out into the darkness. His hand encountered something soft and more than a little gooey.

'Take your fingers out of my nose,' Kate said, her voice sounding more nasal than usual.

'Sorry,' said Cedric. He hastily withdrew his hand and wiped it on his shirt.

'I know we're close, but that's taking it a bit too far,' Kate continued. 'Friends shake hands, maybe even give each other a peck on the cheek …'

'I said I was sorry,' Cedric said sulkily. Then the oddness of their predicament hit him. 'What are you doing here?' he asked.

'Oh, y'know, just some shopping, wondering whether I should go and get my hair done or maybe just relax and go for a cup of coffee … what do you think I'm doing here? I was kidnapped.'

'Kidnapped,' Cedric repeated, letting the word swirl around in his confused mind for a moment.

'Yes, my genius detective. Wait, why are you acting like it's a surprise? Why else would you be here if you didn't know I was kidnapped? I presume you found out where I was, got overpowered by my captors and then they stuffed you into this box with me.'

'Ah ... I ... well ... funny story ...' he began, before trailing off lamely.

'You *didn't know* I was missing?' Kate said, her voice sounding deeper, more booming and more unpleasant than it usually did. And let's be honest, it didn't sound melodic, not even on a good day. Birds wept when they realised their wonderful songs existed in the same universe as Kate's voice.

'Of course I knew you were missing. How could I not?' Cedric blustered, then decided to go with the truth. She was a big girl and he didn't want her to stay angry with him, especially when they were in a confined space and he had nowhere to run and hide. 'No, I didn't know.'

'But how did you find me then?'

'Ahm ...'

Cedric waited while Kate's brain caught up with the way the conversation was going.

'I don't believe it,' she gasped.

'Kate ...'

'Just tell me what happened, Cedric Murphy,' she snapped.

Cedric was glad that the darkness prevented her from seeing how embarrassed he was. 'Do I have to?' he replied in a small voice. He could sense her rising anger even in the suffocating silence. 'I got beaten up. Just a stroke of luck that I woke up here with you.'

'A stroke of *bad* luck. So, both of us have been kidnapped,' Kate sighed. 'Wow. That's depressing. And it makes our detective agency look really useless.'

Cedric decided now wasn't the right time to let her know she was no longer a part of the agency. 'I do know why we're here, if that's any consolation,' he said.

'Good, I was hoping you'd say something about that. Because that's what's really important right now. Explanations.'

Cedric got what she was saying. Better to escape first, then they could worry about why they'd been taken hostage. Yeah, she has a good head on her shoulders, has old Kate. Let's hope it stays there, he thought with a shudder. If it was The Ghost who was after them, then he was certain that something unpleasant lay in their future. Wasn't that always the way with these evil villain types? Not once did they say, 'You know what, I think I've gone a little bit over the top there with all that killing and maiming stuff. Of all the paths I could have chosen in life, I don't know why I picked that one. My mum wanted me to become an accountant, but you know what it's like: you kill one person, then another, and before you know it, it's become a habit. A bad one admittedly, but a habit nonetheless. It seems cruel to torture you now, so for a change of pace I'm going to let you go free. Off you go, you little scamps.' That never happened, did it? No, there was nothing else for it. They were going to have to get out of there by themselves. And fast. He decided to be upbeat for Kate's sake even though he was a cynical pessimist by nature.

'Don't worry, Kate. I'm going to get us out of here,' Cedric said.

'Thanks, I was terrified there for a minute, but now that I know you're on the case all my worries have magically disappeared. It hardly matters that you didn't even notice your own assistant was missing, or that you got captured quicker than a particularly stupid mouse being pursued by a clever cat in a well-lit room. Why would that be a concern? You'll sort everything out. Why, my poor little female heart is all aflutter with gratitude. Whatever would I do without you, Cedric Murphy?'

Ah, he thought, almost dreamily. One hundred percent pure sarcasm. He'd missed it.

'It's good to be with you again, Kate,' he said.

Kate punched him in the ear. 'Stop being such a wimp.'

As Cedric checked for signs of blood he was sure she muttered: 'Good to be with you again too, Ced.'

He smiled briefly.

'Do you have any idea where we are?' he asked.

'A wooden box. That's as much as I've been able to determine,' she said.

'Like a coffin?'

'It'd want to be a pretty big coffin to take two lumps like us,' she said with a chuckle.

There was a sudden silence and when she spoke again there was a note of panic in her voice. 'What if it is a coffin? Oh, Ced, what if they've buried us alive?'

'No, look. Just above your head. I can see little chinks of light. And we're breathing freely, so there must be fresh air getting in here somehow.'

'You're right,' she said, a little calmer. 'Sorry, I haven't smoked a cigar in at least a day. You know how my nerves get at me when I haven't had my smoke.'

'Yeah, you're a barrel of laughs.'

'I remember what you were like when you were on that diet. A psychotic hippopotamus would have been better company,' Kate said.

'OK, we're both horrible when things aren't going our way, but can we stop arguing and get out of here so we can be horrible to the people who really deserve it?'

'Agreed. Now that there's two of us here, maybe we can try kicking our way out.'

'Subtle plan,' said Cedric.

'You got a better one?'

He racked his brain. Nuts. Nothing.

'Yeah, I thought so,' Kate said. 'We start kicking on three.'

Cedric drew his aching knees up to his chest.

'One,' she said.

Kwwwakkk. A scraping sound coming from some-where outside their wooden prison. As if someone was moving something out there. Cedric tried to put it out of his mind. Focus, he told himself. We might only get one shot at this.

'Two.'

The sound was growing louder now and Cedric heard a voice and a low moaning.

'Three.'

·◆·

Colm had expected his journey in the boot of the car to be very uncomfortable and he wasn't disappointed. He'd been thrown into all four corners of the dark and dank space as the car had turned left and right, sped up and slowed down. He'd given up counting the amount of bruises he'd received once he'd reached seven. He felt every bump in the road, but he knew that now wasn't the time to feel sorry for himself. If he was going to get everyone out of this situation he would have to do something. And quickly. But short of leaping out of the boot of a moving car, he didn't know what that something could be.

It had only taken McGrue a couple of minutes to overpower Colm and his friends. It was embarrassing to have been subdued so quickly, but then McGrue had moved swiftly, and his punches had been quite persuasive. Lauryn and The Brute were now sitting in the back seat of the car being held in place by Pretty Boy and Uggo, who had been happy to accept the bounty hunter's authority once they'd seen what he could do, while Colm had for some reason been given different accommodation. From the brief snippets of conversation he'd heard before he'd been bundled into the boot, Colm reckoned that Boris, the wiry man, had paid for his mistake in letting them get away at Colm's house. Paid with his life. Still, he wasn't worried about Boris. He had plenty of other things to worry about.

His brain was in overdrive, trying to figure out what to do next. He wondered where they were going – the logical assumption was that they were being taken to The Ghost, but he wasn't sure how logical The Ghost's plans were. If they *were* being taken to The Ghost then presumably he was going to kill them, and how could a twelve-year-old boy stop him? Plus it was pretty clear at this point that The Ghost had Colm's parents and Colm knew that if the criminal mastermind threatened them he would do whatever he was told. The same went for The Brute and Lauryn. From what he could figure out it looked like The Ghost held all the cards and Colm couldn't see a way of getting himself and everyone else safely out of this mess.

He was so frustrated that he let out a roar. Just for the sake of roaring. To try and get rid of some of the anger and the stress in order to calm down and think clearly. The pressure was really getting to him. People often moaned that the teenage years were the most difficult, but if Colm's life was anything to go by, being twelve wasn't exactly a stroll by the seaside either.

The car hit a pothole and Colm's head thumped against the floor of the boot. He tried to blank out the jolts of pain, the car sickness that threatened to overcome him and the feeling of misery and terror that wanted to wrap itself round him like a cashmere cloak and smother his thoughts. He took a couple of deep breaths. He had to focus. He may not have prepared himself physically like Lauryn, but he'd spent a long time obsessing about the Lazarus Key, The Ghost and *The Book of Dread*. It had taken up too much of his life, but he'd done it for a moment just like this. He had to prove to himself that he hadn't wasted all that time in the library. He needed to sift through all the information and pick out the bits that were useful.

What had he learned? That there were three keys and he'd destroyed one. If he was in The Ghost's position and he was planning a revenge worse than death for his enemies, he'd find the other keys and use them. Most of the stories claimed they were buried in hidden tombs thousands of miles away, with only a sketchy record of their location. However, he guessed that a super-rich criminal wouldn't have any problem using all his resources to have them located and then fund an expedition to retrieve them.

What was the next logical step? Gather up all the people who were involved that night and make them pay. His parents had been there and although they had spent their time locked in a room for the whole thing, The Ghost wouldn't care about that. They had been captured. At least he had to assume so. The Brute, Lauryn, Lauryn's mum and the Prof had met the same fate. But then why had The Brute's mum and stepfather been taken – they hadn't been involved at all. And that detective – what was his part in all of this? He'd helped them twice now. Why? He didn't come across as the helpful sort. What reason would he have otherwise? Private detectives didn't detect for the fun of it, they did it for money. So, who was paying him to investigate and how had he avoided being captured up to that point? Presumably The Ghost wanted revenge against him too. It was a real brain mangler.

The car must have zoomed over a hill because suddenly Colm was thrown in the air. His upward trajectory was only halted by the collision between his nose and the boot's steel sheeting. He landed on his back with a pain in his shoulder and a brand new idea in his head.

Maybe Cedric Murphy had been paid to help the rat-faced man find the key! That would explain how he'd got involved first time around. That's why he had arrived at the hotel in the middle of the night. He'd found out the key's location for Ratters and given him directions. But when he had seen that the man was willing to hurt children, he must have felt guilty and decided to swap sides. It was the only explanation. The only one Colm could think of anyway. Did that make

Cedric Murphy good or bad? It was hard to tell, but it didn't really matter either way now. He'd risked his own life to help them back at the house, so clearly he was on their side this time. Which could be handy later, if he was still alive.

It felt like all the pieces of the puzzle were beginning to fall into place. The only problem was the jigsaw they formed was a picture of him and his family in terrible danger. Also, figuring out what The Ghost was up to, if he was right about the plan, wasn't quite the same as being in a position to stop him from doing it. One thing was for certain: being stuck in the boot of a car driven by a goon wasn't helping his case.

The car screeched to a halt. The engine was switched off and the rattling ceased. Colm heard a door open, then footsteps. Muffled sounds in the night. A girl's voice protesting. That must be Lauryn. If they hurt her he would … what? What could he do when he was stuck here?

The voices drifted away. No more footsteps. Everything was quiet now. Too quiet. He tried to concentrate on an escape plan, but his mind didn't seem to want to go down that road. He had nothing. But he couldn't just give up, so he began kicking against the metal above him. Again and again and again. It didn't work. It hardly even made a dent.

He was on the verge of giving up when the boot opened. Colm's eyes were well adjusted to the darkness and he easily made out the features of the man standing above him, although he couldn't see any of his surroundings. To his surprise it wasn't one of the men who had taken him. He was slim and pale. He was wrapped up in a winter coat and wore a beanie hat that was pulled down so low it almost covered his eyes.

'You still alive,' the man said matter-of-factly.

'I think so. Who are you?' Colm asked.

'I am Alexander. I seek revenge. I help you. You help me. We move fast.'

Twenty-One

Colm could hardly believe his good fortune. Of course he was still in the boot of the car and was being flung around again as it was being driven at high speed, but Alexander finding him like that had been a huge stroke of luck. They'd only had a couple of minutes to talk as the tall Russian was anxious to get on the move before McGrue and the other two goons returned from wherever they had taken Lauryn and The Brute, but in that short time Alexander had explained that he was a mercenary who had been in Transylvania trying to uncover one of the Lazarus Keys. He'd barely escaped with his life and his colleagues had been killed by one of the undead, but Alexander had managed to make it to Dublin and was here to take revenge on The Ghost. Even better, the Russian knew where The Ghost was hiding out. Colm didn't know what he was going to do when he met The Ghost, but at least he'd be a lot safer with Alexander on his side.

Then, as the adrenaline from escaping wore off and Colm's euphoria ebbed away, he began to wonder about a few things: How had Alexander managed to find him? And why did he want him to stay in the boot? He'd said it was because if Colm was spotted the goons would soon be on his trail and that made some kind of sense, but still, they'd left the goons behind and even if they were chasing them wouldn't they recognise the car registration number? Plus, how had Alexander managed to track down a master criminal so easily? And was it really a good idea for one man and a young boy to be racing towards such a dangerous man with no real plan or idea of what they were going to do?

As he thought about all of this a sliver of doubt seeped into Colm's mind and he wondered if he had just gone from the frying pan into the fire.

·◆·

The car had come to a stop. The man who was calling himself Alexander got out. For a moment he felt weak and leaned against the car door breathing deeply.

'Not feeling too good, huh?' said a voice.

'You,' said the impostor who was The Ghost.

He was seeing his brother again. Another hallucination. The doctors had said they would become more frequent the closer he got to death. There wasn't much time left now.

'If I was the one who was dying, I wouldn't be spending time driving a car around in circles only to end up in the exact same spot I'd started from.'

The Ghost glanced at the shopping centre and smiled. His brother was right. This was almost exactly the same place McGrue had left the car. He'd have to track down the bounty hunter later, when he was feeling like himself again. The man had done exactly as he'd requested, but The Ghost didn't like witnesses. There were too many people who'd seen him in the last few days. Dying was making his work sloppy. In the past, he'd have killed McGrue on the spot, but he'd already ended a life tonight and his strength was waning. That Russian who had managed to follow Camus all the way from Transylvania had been a tough one. Must have been to go to all that effort. He'd almost got the better of The Ghost. Almost.

'Lost in a reverie?' the rat-faced man asked.

'Stop annoying me. You're not real.'

'Yet you're still talking to me.'

He was right. Why was that? He rarely talked to anyone made of flesh and bone, yet here he was talking to the ghost of his brother. The Ghost talking to a ghost.

There was a moment's silence and then the rat-faced man said, 'I get it now.'

'What?'

'The driving around in circles. It's for the Abbatage. The participant must come willingly to the ritual, otherwise it won't work. You've tricked the boy into thinking you're on his side. So he's chosen to come here with you.'

'You always were slow on the uptake,' The Ghost sneered.

'You'd better hurry. Dawn is less than an hour away. From the dullness in your eyes, it looks like you won't be strong enough to wait another day.'

'Then I'd better get started,' The Ghost said.

•◆•

Colm was confused. He could hear someone speaking out there. It sounded a little like Alexander, but at the same time it didn't. There was only one voice. Was he talking to himself?

The boot opened and The Ghost reached in, holding his hand out for Colm to take.

'You come with me?' he asked, expertly faking a Russian accent. 'You are willing participant?'

Colm wasn't certain it was the right thing to do, but what other choice did he have? This Alexander looked dangerous. His eyes were cold, almost lifeless. It was also the way he held himself, the way he spoke, or was it something else? He was certain he was missing something, but he couldn't quite put his finger on what it might be.

'You bet,' Colm said, feigning cheeriness. He grabbed the man's hand. The fingers were icy to the touch and, just for a moment, an image of death flickered in Colm's mind, as if the man had sent him a signal. With a growing sense of unease, he clambered out of the boot.

He found himself in front of a building that looked very familiar. 'The shopping centre? The Ghost is in the shopping centre? Why would he be there?' But Colm had the answer to his own question before The Ghost replied. 'Of course! This is where my dad works. He's holding my parents here. That's it, isn't it?'

'Yes,' said The Ghost as they walked through the mostly empty car park and around the back of the centre, which was half-illuminated by the full moon.

The shopping centre was huge and relatively new, only three years old. During the day it was packed with shoppers, but at night it looked bleak, like a giant empty shell. Colm could hear an occasional car pass by on the main road almost half a kilometre away, but otherwise it was as if they were in the middle of nowhere.

'What about the others? Where are they?'

'We stop Ghost. Rescue parents. Then we find others, OK?'

'OK,' Colm agreed. 'But you have a plan, right? I mean it's The Ghost, the most dangerous criminal in the world. We're not going to go in there without a plan.'

'I have plan,' The Ghost said.

'What is it?'

The Ghost smiled at Colm. He didn't smile very often and it showed. It sent chills through Colm's soul.

'No time to explain. Come with me now.'

Colm stopped dead. 'No. I'm not going up against The Ghost without knowing what our plan is.' Something's definitely wrong, he thought, very wrong. His heart had begun to pound and he felt sick to the pit of his stomach. What was that phrase the man had used before he'd got out of the boot of the car? A willing participant. Colm had thought it sounded strange, but he'd put it down to the fact that Alexander was speaking a language foreign to him.

'You figure it out?' The Ghost asked, but Colm barely heard him, still lost in thought. Willing participant. He'd heard that phrase before, but where? No, not heard it, read it. The Lazarus Key notes. Abbatage. The ceremony to end all ceremonies. The one that would give the holder of the keys immortality. It needed a willing participant.

Him.

He looked at the man again. 'Did you say something?'

'I say nothing.'

Every last cell in his body sent a signal to his brain

telling him to get out of there as fast as he could.

'You know, maybe this isn't such a great idea. You and me against The Ghost? I don't think that's going to work out too well for either of us. We need back up,' Colm said.

'Back up?' The man was trying his best to stay calm, but Colm could sense the anger bubbling just under the surface.

'The gardaí. We should ring them.'

'They won't believe. Then it's too late.'

'Too late for what?'

The Ghost rubbed his temples. The pain behind his eyes was back and it was worse than ever. His brother was right – his time was coming to an end. He had to hurry. He had to start the ceremony.

'You can go in if you want, but I think I'm going to ...'

'You're going nowhere,' said The Ghost. The Russian accent was suddenly gone.

Colm turned and ran. He didn't even know where he was going and he didn't care, just as long as he put some distance between himself and this man.

The man.

It was The Ghost, Colm realised, it had to be.

He pumped his arms, trying desperately to move faster. He couldn't hear any footsteps behind him, only his own on the silky, black tarmac. That had to be good. Perhaps the man wasn't following him. He wasn't going to look back and check. He just had to keep running. When he was safe, he could figure out what to do.

But then he felt a sharp pain in his head and everything faded into black.

Twenty-Two

It took a few moments for Lauryn's eyes to adjust to the semi-darkness. She wondered what had happened to her. I must have been knocked out, she thought, although she didn't remember getting an injection or a blow to the head. She realised she was lying on a floor. The cool tiles pressed against her cheek. It was actually comfortable there, which she knew meant she was exhausted. It's not as if a tiled floor is the type of bed you'd choose for yourself. She forced herself to sit up. Her head began to swim.

She heard a groan of pain coming from her right-hand side. It was excruciating, but she managed to turn her head and saw The Brute was face down on the ground only a couple of metres away.

'Hey, Mikey, wake up. We gotta get moving,' she said.

The Brute groaned again. He rubbed the back of his head. A bruise the size of a ping-pong ball had formed just above the top of his neck.

'I don't feel too good,' he mumbled. 'Where are we?'

Lauryn stood up.

'It looks like we're in some sort of store.'

She let her body go limp, trying to relax enough to shake off the aches and pains. The Brute struggled to his feet.

'What happened to us?' he asked.

'Dunno. The last thing I remember is those guys dragging us out of the car. Why would they put us in here though?'

'I have no idea,' The Brute said. He usually didn't.

She looked around. She was right, they were in some kind of store, more specifically, a two euro shop. The shelves were stacked with cheap goods of all kinds: sweets, plastic guns, cleaning products, and what seemed like a million other things.

She moved forward fearlessly, checking out every part of the shop by the light on her watch until she was satisfied that there was no one else in there. She returned to find The Brute by the counter halfway through a packet of extra-cheesy crisps.

'You're eating? At a time like this?'

'I'm starving, girl. I haven't had a proper meal in like, twelve hours,' he said, cheese dust spilling down the front of his Eagles t-shirt.

'I hope you paid for them.'

'I'm out of cash. I'll leave an IOU.'

He was regretting choosing the crisps though. If Lauryn wanted to kiss him later his breath would probably stink. Now that he thought of it, maybe being trapped in here wasn't such a bad thing. It would give them some alone time.

'You're a strange kind of guy,' Lauryn said as she began looking for the main light switch. She nipped behind the counter. It seemed to be the most likely place to find it. Back home they always seemed to control everything in shops from behind the counter.

The Brute barely noticed what she was up to; he was still lost in thought. Yeah, y'know, this place is actually kind of romantic, he was thinking as Lauryn found the switch and flicked it on. The fluorescent lights began to buzz and flicker as they came to life. The light was harsh and made everything seem a little too real, killing the romantic mood The Brute had been hoping would continue. Of course, if the lights hadn't done it, the mood would have been broken by the member of the undead who was on the other side of the shop's front door.

·◆·

When Cedric had reached the count of three, he'd kicked out with everything he'd got. His feet smashed against the roof of their prison and the wood began to creak.

'That was a good start,' he'd wheezed as some splinters nestled in his ear. 'You ready to kick again?'

'More ready than you are,' Kate said.

'We'll see about that.'

It had taken them ten minutes to break free of the box. They had both been surprised to find that they were in a clothes shop.

'What's going on here, Ced?'

'I don't know. And before you point it out, yes, I'm aware that I'm a detective.'

'A clothes shop?' Kate said. 'Who keeps someone prisoner in a clothes shop?'

'Someone who thinks we have terrible taste in clothing and wants us to dress more sharply,' Cedric suggested.

Kate ignored the idiotic remark. She found the switches she was looking for and turned them on.

'Wow,' she said, as the shop was flooded with light, revealing aisle after aisle of clothing. 'This is an expensive place. They've got some really good quality stuff here.'

'I thought you didn't have any interest in clothes,' Cedric said.

'I've as much interest in clothes as you have in taking a shower,' Kate said, examining a beige cashmere jumper.

Huh? Was she saying he stank? Cedric sneakily smelled his armpits. Phew. It *was* fairly unpleasant.

'Kate, I've uncovered a clue.'

'What is it?'

'Remember the way, when we were trapped in the box, that I said it sounded like there was someone moaning and groaning out there and you said you didn't hear anything? Well, take a look.'

He pointed to the front door.

On the other side of the glass an undead man stood in the hallway, staring in. Cedric looked smug.

'Yeah, good one, Ced. This is really the right time for your "I told you so" face,' Kate said.

·◆·

Lauryn finished packing the Peppa Pig schoolbag that had been designed for someone at least ten years younger than she was. She zipped it up and slung it over her right shoulder. It was so small that if she'd tried to put it over both shoulders it would have ripped apart.

'Well?' Lauryn asked when The Brute returned.

'There's some kind of digital door lock on the back door. Unless you're a code-cracking genius, then it looks like we could be spending a lot of time in here.'

'What are you talking about?'

He glanced at the undead outside, pawing at the clear glass. It had been joined by another – this one was wearing a security guard's uniform. Other than that they were very similar. Blank eyes. Slack jaws. Drool dripping down their chins. They stumbled forward banging against the glass as if they were controlled by a three-year-old with a remote. He wondered why the light wasn't affecting them. They were supposed to be bothered by light, weren't they?

'We can't leave while those lads are outside. As long as we stay in here, we'll be safe,' The Brute said. 'There's plenty to eat and drink and someone will turn up to rescue us eventually.'

'And what about your cousin?'

'Colm? He'll be fine. He's well able to look after himself.'

He didn't like the look Lauryn gave him. It seemed to be a combination of disgust and … no, disgust pretty much covered it.

'You know I'm joking, right?' he lied.

'Really? What you said was funny? I guess I just don't get the Irish sense of humour.'

'Oh yeah, if Colm was here he'd be cracking up at what I said. So what's the plan?'

'Good. That's more like it. Right, what we're going to do is this – you're going to open the doors and I'm going to launch myself at the two dead dudes out there. They seem kind of dopey, so they won't expect us to attack. I knock them down, then you drag me off them and we look for Colm.'

'Right, good plan ... just a couple of problems with it. Like, what if they just grab you and try to eat you?'

'It's a chance I'm willing to take.'

'Fair enough, but let me put it another way – WHAT IF THEY GRAB YOU AND TRY TO EAT YOU?'

'Fortune favours the brave.'

'I've never understood that phrase. Anyway, we can't do it. The doors are locked. I'd love to open them, but ...'

'That's OK, I can pick door locks.'

'Of course you can,' The Brute sighed. 'Excuse me.'

He brushed past her and ducked beneath the counter.

'What are you doing?'

'Just a hunch. You'd be surprised how often people leave spare keys in obvious places ... a-ha.' When he re-emerged he was holding a little silver key.

'Is that ...' Lauryn began.

'The spare key.'

'Why would anyone leave a spare key in a shop? It doesn't make any sense.'

'Who cares?' The Brute said.

'Right, you unlock the door and I'll hit 'em hard.'

'I can't do it, Lauryn. I can't unlock the door.'

'If you're not going to do it, give it to me.'

The Brute held the key aloft, just out of reach. 'Sorry, I can't let you go out there. It's madness.'

'Every second we spend here yapping is a second wasted. Colm is in danger. And if the guy behind this kidnapping is The Ghost you can bet he has something planned for us too. I'm not someone who can sit around waiting for something to happen to me. I'm going out that door whether you help me or not and I'm not going to waste valuable minutes picking the lock.'

'You'll have to if I have the key,' he replied.

Lauryn punched him in the stomach. He wasn't expecting it and he doubled over in pain. She plucked the key from his fingers.

'Good one,' The Brute wheezed. There aren't too many people who are impressed when you punch them in the belly, but he was one of the few.

'Sorry, I didn't want to do that, but ...'

'I know,' he said, catching his breath. 'It's all right. I'll help you.'

'Do you mean it?' Lauryn asked.

He did. He had to help her. He couldn't let her go out there by herself. Anyway, he liked to think of himself as a man of action and it was time to act, even if it meant facing some half-deads or undeads or vamumzompires.

'Glad you're on board,' Lauryn said, handing him back the key.

The Brute moved to the door and put the key in the lock. His heart thumped in his chest.

'One thing – I'm going to hit those guys, not you.'

Lauryn began to raise an objection, but The Brute cut her off with a wave of his hand.

'It's not 'cos I think you can't. Your punch to my stomach was almost perfect. I know you're tough, but it's just that I'm bigger. It makes more sense.'

'OK,' Lauryn said with a smile. 'Just give me a second.'

She took the schoolbag off her shoulder, unzipped it and reached in.

'I hope you paid for that stuff,' The Brute said.

'I left them an IOU,' Lauryn replied with a half-smile.

The Brute noticed that the hand that held the key was shaking like jelly on a windy day. Just pretend those guys are a couple of rugby centres, he told himself. You've got the ball and you've got to burst through them.

The undead stared in at him. They didn't understand what was happening, their brains only told them one thing – to kill anyone they encountered. Their limbs flailed against the glass.

Ugliest centres I ever saw, The Brute thought.

Lauryn nodded at him. She was ready. It was time.

He turned the key in the lock and wrenched the door open.

The undead stumbled forward into the shop as Lauryn flung something in their direction.

A bright yellow frisbee caught the first one right on the nose. Its head jerked back and it tottered for a moment before slipping on the tiled floor and hitting the ground. Its body began to spasm.

The second frisbee she threw – a pink one – sailed harmlessly over the creature in the security guard's uniform. It flew out into the hallway.

The Brute heard Lauryn swear as he threw himself forward, grabbing the creature around the waist and bringing it down with a perfectly timed tackle. There wasn't time to congratulate himself. He sprang to his feet, leaped over the still prone first creature and out into the hallway. Lauryn sprinted after him, but as she jumped over the two creatures lying on the ground, the first one began to rise, moaning horrifically. Its hand reached out and grabbed her foot, tripping her up. She landed on her shoulder, crying out as the pain shot through her.

The Brute was by her side immediately. He grabbed her wrist and tried to pull her up, but the creature was still clinging on to her foot, so he took hold of her under the arms and started to pull her out of the shop. A brief tug of war developed and as this was going on the security guard drew itself up. It saw its chance.

The Brute's eyes were bulging with the effort as he dragged Lauryn out through the door. The undead wouldn't let go and he was having to drag both of them along the ground. It was exhausting and the decaying stench given off by the two creatures was almost unbearable. It was so rank it burned the inside of his nostrils.

'You go. Leave me here, I can fight them off,' Lauryn cried.

'That line only works in films,' The Brute grunted, continuing to pull.

The undead security man, which had worked its way around the bodies on the ground, now swung an arm towards The Brute, its hot, clammy fingers clawing against the teenager's sweaty face. The second creature pulled itself forward, using Lauryn as a climbing rope. She saw the way its eyes changed the closer it got to her beating heart. The dullness became a gleam, like an animal that's just realised it's feeding time. She kicked out, wriggling like a snake on fast forward, but the creature hung on grimly.

'Let me go,' The Brute shouted.

Lauryn hadn't time to look at him. Was he talking to her?

'Lauryn. Let me go,' he repeated.

Was this guy deserting her? So what if he is, I can take these two creatures by myself, Lauryn thought, even though deep down she knew that she couldn't. No matter how often she kicked out at the one on her leg it wouldn't let go.

She released the grip she hadn't realised she had on The Brute. He removed his arms from under hers, shrugged off the security creature and ran farther out into the hallway.

He really is going to desert me, Lauryn thought, as she heard his footsteps move rapidly away.

But he wasn't leaving her behind. He was just backing

up to get a bit of momentum going. He reached the wall on the far side of the hall, turned and ran back towards the shop. He stuck out an arm at a ninety degree angle from his body and kept it straight and strong. He sprinted faster than he'd ever sprinted before. The security undead looked at him, confused, then the creature's world went black as The Brute's arm caught it hard on the chest, clothes-lining it and sending it into a flip that would have won a bronze at an Undead Olympic Gymnasts' competition.

The Brute left the ground and swan-dived forward, propelled by his speed, and landed right on top of the second creature, flattening it.

The creature let out a moan of pain and released its hold on Lauryn. She got to her feet as The Brute jumped back to his and beat his chest in defiance.

'Don't ever mess with the "dude",' he shouted at the prostrate undead.

'You can gloat later,' Lauryn said, slinging the schoolbag over her shoulder again. 'Let's get out of here before they recover.'

'*If* they recover,' The Brute smirked.

But he still dragged the two bodies into the shop and

locked the door behind him so that the creatures were trapped.

'Now let's finish this,' Lauryn said.

She took The Brute's hand, which almost caused him to faint with excitement, and they began to run along the darkened hall.

Twenty-Three

'Hey you, open the door,' Kate shouted at the undead creature outside. She banged against the door with her fist. 'Wait a second, I recognise him. He's the guy who kidnapped me.'

She was right. The undead was Wiry Boris. Although the part of him that had been Boris, the unpleasantness that had been his personality, seemed to have gone on holiday. He walked into the glass door again and again, driven by a desire to kill. No more getting the others to do his dirty work. This time he was going to do it all by himself.

'I know him too,' Cedric said. 'I punched him on the nose.'

'I threw him into a dish of cat food,' Kate said. 'I'd say that hurt more than one of your punches.'

'It's not a competition, Kate.'

'He doesn't look like himself. I mean, he's still creepy, but it's a different sort of creepiness.'

The creature that was once Wiry Boris bumped into the door again, then tottered backwards, leaving a trail of snot and slime on the glass.

'Disgusting,' Kate muttered to herself.

'He reminds me of ...' Cedric began.

'What?'

'That Hugh DeLancey-O'Brien creature. The one I helped dispose of in the woods that night. He's acting a bit like him.'

'Is he a zombie? 'Cos I don't like zombies. They eat brains, don't they?' Kate said.

'No, that's a popular myth. The first brain-eaters only appeared in a film in the late 1960s–'

'Are you giving me a history lesson? Listen to me, Cedric Murphy – I don't care about myths. I want to know what he'll do if he gets in here.'

'I don't know.'

'Then shut your trap about the 1960s and all that

rubbish.'

'I presume he'll kill us in some way. Probably grue-somely. I mean the man who captured us is unlikely to put the undead outside as guards if they're just going to let us pass by. No, it'll be horrifying and gruesome, all right.'

'You really have no idea of how to reassure someone, do you?' Kate said.

'You're big enough to handle the truth,' Cedric replied.

That was true enough.

'If our kidnapper put us here and has given us an undead guard, then that means he wants to stop us going outside. When somebody wants me to do something, I really, really want to do the opposite, no matter how scary it is,' Kate said.

'You're saying you want us to break out of here, aren't you?'

'You bet your sweet bippy that's what I'm saying.'

'All the doors are locked,' Cedric said.

'Then we'll have to bust our way out.'

'Bust our way out? You sound like—'

Kate gave him one of her trademark withering glares. 'What? What do I sound like?'

'You sound like a woman with a plan,' Cedric said with a gulp. 'Let's bust out of here. I can't wait to get out there and face that creature.'

'Those creatures,' Kate corrected him as the undead Pretty Boy and Uggo joined their hated colleague outside the door.

'This just gets better and better,' Cedric sighed.

'Shhh, do you hear that?'

The sound of footsteps outside. Somebody was running down the hallway. Kate's jaw dropped open as The Brute and Lauryn raced past, skilfully dodging the outstretched arms of the former goons.

'Was that ...'

'Oh yeah, I forgot to mention them. Funny story,' Cedric said.

Kate wasn't listening. The three undead creatures had lost interest in getting into the shop. They turned and began to amble after Lauryn and The Brute. They were ten times slower than the teenagers, but they only had one thing on their minds and they wouldn't be stopped.

·•◆•·

The security control centre was brightly lit. There were two chairs in front of a large bank of blank computer screens. Colm sat in one of them.

His eyes flickered open.

'You're back,' The Ghost said without a hint of emotion.

Colm tried to shake away the cloud of fuzziness that enveloped his mind.

'Where am I?'

'It doesn't matter.'

Colm got to his feet. He felt a little unsteady, but stronger than he expected. He was doing his best to remain calm. He needed to think clearly, now more than ever. Did the man really think that he could make himself immortal? Eighteen months ago Colm would have laughed at the idea, but he'd seen a lot of strange things since then.

'You won't get away with this,' he said.

The Ghost ignored him. He reached under a desk and took out a wooden shield about one metre high and half a metre across at its widest point. It was covered with intricate wooden carvings of horrific scenes, all depicting people dying in a stomach-churning manner. There were three small holes at its centre. For a moment

Colm & The Ghost's Revenge •

The Ghost seemed to be consumed by it, as if it was a thing of beauty. He ran his fingers across the wooden surface, lightly caressing it.

Colm's eyes were scanning the room, searching for something he could use, anything that might help him to escape. The only door was triple locked. Two deadlocks and a thick, iron bolt. Was it to stop Colm getting out or someone from getting in? Maybe both. The Ghost was far stronger than Colm, but if he wanted to stop him getting out ... did that mean the Abbatage ceremony made him weak? Possibly, but it wasn't something Colm could rely upon. There wasn't much else in there. Other than the desks and chairs and computers. Except that microphone which he assumed was used for announcements, but what good was that?

The Ghost handed him the shield. 'Hold this.'

'What if I say no?' Colm asked, stuffing his hands in his pockets.

The Ghost gently laid the shield against the security system console and pressed a button on the control panel. Two of the computer screens flickered to life. When the images appeared Colm gasped. Each screen showed a picture of one of the shops in the shopping centre and even though the lights weren't on in there, the cameras were on night vision. The images were clear enough for Colm to recognise the people locked inside. His mother was in one shop, his father in another. And outside each one he could see shadowy figures at the shop door. Pawing at the glass, pounding in some cases. Trying to break in and devour the people inside.

'You're a monster,' Colm shouted.

'The glass is strong, but my army of the undead is strong too. Within minutes they will have broken in and your parents will not be strong enough to fight them off. They will die. Unpleasantly.'

He looked down at the control panel and flicked the switches for another couple of screens. As they flickered on Colm saw The Brute and Lauryn, or some people who looked very like them, running along the hallway. The Ghost hadn't looked up, but as soon as he did he would see the two escapees. I can't let that happen, Colm thought, I have to distract him.

He picked up a manual from the desk beside him and threw it at The Ghost. The man easily batted it away, but it was enough to draw his attention away from the monitors. 'Enough, we have no time for your childish temper tantrums.'

'Why are you doing this to my parents? It's me you want.'

'Your parents are nothing to me, but as long as I have them you'll do what I tell you. You know of the Abbatage ceremony?'

Upon hearing the word Abbatage Colm pretended to faint. It was the oldest trick in the book. He collapsed theatrically, knocking the shield from where it lay against the security console. The Ghost caught it before it hit the ground.

'Stop playing games, boy,' he growled. 'Get up.'

Colm opened his eyes and did his best to feign embarrassment at being caught out. He grabbed the console and hauled himself to his feet. As The Ghost was examining the shield carefully for damage, Colm hit the microphone switch with his elbow.

·◆·

'We're never going to find him,' The Brute panted as they jogged up the stairs.

'You don't believe in positive thinking, do you?' Lauryn said.

'I'm Irish. Most of us prefer to grumble and we love to expect the worst.'

They reached the top of the stairs. Lauryn stopped and unzipped the schoolbag. She reached in and produced a torch.

'Man, that bag has everything we need,' The Brute said, impressed.

Lauryn switched on the torch. They took a couple of steps forward and leaned over the railing, which gave them a view of the black and white tiled floor below. There were plenty of people moving down there. Unfortunately, they were all citizens of the country of Undead.

'Where are they all coming from?' Lauryn wondered.

'I'm more concerned with where they're going.'

'Huh?'

'They seem to be heading this way.'

'We can outrun them,' Lauryn said.

'We can for now. But we're going to tire eventually,' The Brute replied. 'Maybe he's not here. Colm, I mean. Just 'cos The Ghost locked us up in a shopping centre with a load of freaky creatures doesn't mean that Colm's here. He could have other plans for him.'

Lauryn thought that The Brute had a point. That didn't mean she was going to admit it, though. She had to believe that Colm was here somewhere, that they were going to rescue him and defeat The Ghost.

'No one has ever performed that ceremony success-fully,' boomed a voice on the public address system. The speakers in the shopping centre crackled, distort-ing the voice slightly, but The Brute would have recog-nised that nasally whine anywhere. It was his cousin.

'Well, it seems Colm is here,' he said.

'And he's still alive,' Lauryn said in an I-told-you-so tone.

But then they heard another voice, a cold, even voice.

'You have a choice,' The Ghost said. 'Either help me with the Abbatage or watch everyone you care about die in a slow and horrible manner.'

His words gave The Brute and Lauryn the creeps.

'He doesn't mean me. Colm doesn't care about me that much. That means I won't be one of the ones dying in a slow and horrible manner,' said The Brute.

'It doesn't mean that at all,' Lauryn replied.

'I know, I was just trying to think positively.'

•◆•

The Ghost grabbed the microphone from Colm's hand and wrenched it from its socket, knocking over a computer screen, sending it crashing to the ground. Shards of monitor glass spilled across the floor.

'What did you hope to achieve by broadcasting our conversation?'

'That's not your concern,' said Colm, as bravely as he could while backing away from The Ghost. He didn't feel brave any longer.

The man stared at him. He threw the microphone at Colm. It caught him on the side of the head. The blow stung, but he tried not to show it. He didn't even flinch.

'Anyway, you can't perform the ceremony. You need three Lazarus Keys and only two still exist,' Colm said. 'We destroyed the third one last year.' On that night, which now seemed like it was centuries ago, Colm had tricked the rat-faced man into swallowing the third key and it had dissolved in the acid in his stomach.

The Ghost turned away for a moment, seemingly unconcerned by Colm's statement. Then he played his hand. He held out a velvet bag. He pulled open the drawstring and Colm saw a small, sparkly object fall into The Ghost's palm, quickly followed by a second one. The keys began to glow. For a moment, despite his certainty that only two remained, he expected the worst. But then his heart leaped. There were two keys. Only two. He almost wept with relief. Then, 'Look closer,' the man said, holding the bag open.

Colm took a step towards him and peered in. There at the bottom of the bag was the third key. It looked smaller than he remembered, pitted and worn, but it was still unmistakably a Lazarus Key.

'But how?' he stammered. 'We destroyed ...' he trailed off, horrified.

'I cut this from your enemy's stomach after his death,' said The Ghost.

'But Drake said it would have been destroyed in seconds.'

'Drake isn't as smart as he likes to think he is.'

'You're sick.'

'More than you know.'

'It won't work,' Colm said. 'It *can't* work. The keys have to be complete to work,' he cried, desperation creeping into his voice.

'It is not the keys that need to be complete, it's the energy they contain. I may only have part of the key, but that is enough. Now all I need is the last energy that flowed into it.'

In a flash, Colm saw what he meant. The last life force to enter the key. The last person to hold it in his hand before it was partly destroyed. In other words – him. Now he understood why the key had become such an obsession. As long as the key survived, even if it was damaged, he was still part of it. His was the energy it had tasted last and on some level he had retained a link to it because of this.

'I won't do it, whatever it is you want me to do. I may have come willingly up to now, but you can't force me to play my part in the ritual,' he cried defiantly. 'I won't allow you to become immortal and carry on doing all the horrible things …'

'Then I will die,' said The Ghost. 'But so will you. And before you do, you will watch this. Look.'

The Ghost pointed a long, slim finger at one of the screens. A hand had broken through the glass in the front door of the shop his mother was in. Colm watched with growing horror as one of the slavering creatures smashed its hands repeatedly against the glass, chipping away more and more each time. That was his mother in there. Terrified. His mother.

'NO', screamed Colm at the screen, but she couldn't hear him.

Twenty-Four

'Where's the control room?' Lauryn asked, as they set off running again. They had to find it. The one with all the CCTV cameras and microphones and stuff like that. That's where the PA system would be, wouldn't it?

'I haven't a clue,' The Brute replied.

They rushed past shop after shop – Jack McD's DVDs; Austin Flowers – Lauryn's boots click-clacking on the floor. In the distance, far behind them, they could hear the wailing of the undead as they continued their slow, steady pursuit of the teenagers.

'Stop,' The Brute called out, as he skidded to a halt. 'Look.'

There was a floor plan of the shopping centre stuck

to the wall behind some perspex glass. A map detailing where all the shops, toilets and car parks were. It was colour-coded and easy to read. Lauryn looked up and down, left and right, letting her eyes drift over every part of the map.

'I can't see the control room anywhere on this,' she said.

The Brute ran his finger over the listings: card shop, toy shop, clothes shops, toilets, newsagents. If he'd wanted to buy a book or a bar of chocolate or pay a visit to the bathroom he'd have no problem finding the right place, but there was nothing to let them know the location of any security or control centre.

'Do you hear something?' Lauryn asked suddenly.

The Brute turned. She was right. There was a banging noise coming from somewhere, like someone pounding on glass. He took off. Three shops farther down he found the source of the noise.

'Shine the light here,' he said, pointing at Murphy's Paw, a pet shop.

On the other side of the front door, amongst the squawking parrots and the more silent snakes and goldfish, were some familiar faces.

'Mom!' Lauryn cried. She grabbed the large silver handle and tried to wrench the door open. It wouldn't budge.

Her mother beamed at her. She looked like a wreck, but she was alive and that was all Lauryn cared about. She wasn't alone – Professor Peter Drake was just behind her.

'Lauryn, what are you doing here? Are you OK?' Lauryn's mother, Marie, shouted through the glass.

'I'm fine, Mom,' Lauryn shouted back, still tugging at the door.

'Thank goodness it's you. We saw the flashlight beam when you were farther down the hallway and we decided to take a calculated risk to attract your attention. Can you get us out of here?'

'Sure! Why didn't you pick the lock, Prof?'

The professor held his hands up in front of him. They were swathed in bandages. 'Our captor must have suspected I had such a talent.'

'Broken?'

'They'll heal, but they're pretty useless right now. Is it …'

Lauryn knew him so well she didn't have to wait for

him to finish the question.

'Yep, The Ghost. He's got us good this time, but we're not beaten yet.'

Two others who had been hiding in the back of the shop came forward when they heard the discussion going on – The Brute's mum and his stepfather, Seanie.

'Ma,' he shouted in delight.

His mother ran to the door. She pressed her face up against the glass. 'My lovely, lovely boy. Are you all right?'

'I'm fine, Ma. You?'

Lauryn saw that The Brute bore a startling resemblance to his mother. If you put a brown curly wig and a dress on the boy, they could have been the same person. She was slightly less muscly and a good deal less orange, but otherwise ...

'I'm fine, Michael. What are you doing in Dublin and why are you out in the middle of the night in a t-shirt? You'll catch your death of cold.'

'I'm fine the way I am,' The Brute replied. He nodded curtly to Seanie, who nodded back.

Lauryn pulled an elasticated headlamp from the schoolbag, put it on, and in seconds was on her knees picking at the lock.

'Lauryn,' The Brute said.

'Don't worry, I'll have your mom out of there in a second.'

'No, it's not that, it's just that those zombies or undead or whatever you call them are getting far too close for my liking.' The Brute shone the torch down the hallway. The light scanned the empty faces of at least ten of the undead. They were no more than forty metres away, slowly closing in on them.

'I'll be quick,' she said.

The Brute wasn't convinced. Even though the creatures were shuffling forward slowly, he didn't think Lauryn was going to be quick enough. The creatures' progress was like that of a tortoise heading towards a rock – interminably slow, but the tortoise was inevitably going to make it because the rock was going nowhere.

'I'm going to check we're all clear in the other direction,' The Brute said.

'Huh?'

'This level we're on – inside the railing, it's like a running track. It runs in a loop. If the undead dudes get closer we'll run away and they'll follow us. We'll do a complete circuit until we end up back here again. I'm guessing they're too thick to realise they could turn around, so it'll take them ages to catch up with us.'

'Good thinking,' Lauryn said, working away on the lock. 'Rats. This one ain't easy. Who'd have thought a pet store needed such heavy security?'

'Michael, where do you think you're going? It's dangerous out there. I've seen those zombie yokes,' The Brute's mother roared through the glass. 'I'm telling you to stay here with me unless you want to be ... grounded.'

'Listen to your mother,' Seanie shouted.

'Don't tell me what to do, you're not my father,' The Brute shouted back. 'And Ma, grounded? You learned that off the telly. Anyway, they're not exactly zombies, they're ...' he said. 'Look, I'll be fine. Please just stay quiet so we can focus and let Lauryn and me sort it out.'

Deirdre loved her son with every last fibre of her being, but even she found it hard to believe he could sort this out. She'd seen his bedroom. He couldn't even sort out putting underpants and socks into a laundry basket.

'OK, I'm just going to take a quick recce in this direction to make sure the coast is clear,' The Brute said, disappearing into the semi-darkness.

'You do that,' Lauryn said.

'Perhaps the boy could just try and escape from the mall and raise the alarm,' the professor shouted.

'Nah,' Lauryn said, her eyes still on the lock. 'He's trying to find his cousin. Remember that kid Colm? We've got to rescue him too.'

'My nephew's out there?' Deirdre asked, but no one paid any attention to her.

'Those creatures are getting very close, Lauryn,' her mother said nervously.

Lauryn looked up again. Twenty metres away.

'I've still got a few seconds. Hey Prof, ever heard of something called Agg ... Add ... Abb–'

Professor Drake's face fell. 'Abbatage?'

'That's the one.'

'It couldn't be. He'd have to have the three Lazarus Keys to perform ...' he said muttering to himself. 'Where did you hear that word?'

'Abba-whatsit? We caught a snippet of a conversation between Colm and the guy we think is The Ghost. What does it mean?'

'If The Ghost performs Abbatage he will become

immortal. He'll be the most powerful man who has ever existed.'

'Since he's pretty much pure evil, I guess that'd be a bad thing, huh?'

'He'll make Vlad the Impaler and Attila the Hun look like errant schoolboys,' Drake said. 'Oh, this is bad. Very, very bad. Worse than bad. It's apocalyptic.'

'Lauryn! The zombies! They're getting closer.'

'Relax, Mom, I got it. How do we stop this Abbatage thing?'

'We have to stop the ceremony. From what I've read, if the ceremony is interrupted then the Abbatage cannot be completed. There's not a whole lot on it. As far as I can ascertain it's only been tried on a handful of occasions many, many centuries ago. I can't say if it worked, but I don't recall meeting any immortals recently.'

'I'll get you guys out of here, then we'll find The Ghost and stop the ceremony,' Lauryn said.

'I admire your optimism, but it's not that simple. The interrupter has to be extremely strong. Mentally, I mean. And there's more.' Professor Drake absent-mindedly stroked his chin, then let out a yelp of pain.

When you have broken hands, chin stroking is not something you should indulge in.

'What about my Michael? He's not going to try and stop this weirdness, is he?' The Brute's mother asked. Seanie wrapped his arms around her and squeezed her tightly.

'Prof, what's the "more" you mentioned?'

'I can't be one hundred percent certain …'

'Prof!'

'The interrupter stops the transfer of immortality. When the keys don't work as one the power is too much for anyone to take. The person performing the ceremony dies.'

'And the interrupter dies too?' Lauryn said.

'No, worse than that. He or she will drift into a living death, slowly becoming a thing rather than a person. A monster of the night.'

A macaw squawked and began to throw itself against the bars of its cage. The other birds joined in.

'Lauryn,' Marie shouted. She thumped her fists against the glass to warn her daughter.

'I said it's OK, Mom. I got it,' Lauryn snapped.

She glanced in the direction of the creatures, the

LED headlamp illuminating their open, slavering jaws. Fifteen, twenty of them. They were right on top of her.

Lauryn's face drained of colour. 'Looks like I haven't got it after all.'

•◆•

The Brute waved the torch left and right, moving as quietly and carefully as he could. The last thing he needed was to accidentally sneak up on one of the undead. He could outrun them certainly, but if one of them appeared out of the darkness and grabbed him … he shuddered at the thought.

Lauryn's voice had grown distant until it was mixed with the wailing of the undead creatures and it was impossible to tell the two sounds apart. Hurry up with that lock, girl, he muttered to himself.

He walked on, trying to make his footsteps as soft and quiet as he could, forgetting that although the undead might not be able to hear him, they'd definitely be able to see the light from his torch.

He reached the end of the row of shops. The walkway curved around, just like he'd said. An ellipse. If he continued walking in that direction, he'd end up back with Lauryn. There was a sign for the toilets just ahead. Then the light picked out a door with the words 'STAFF ONLY'. That looked promising. It might lead to the control room.

He twisted the door knob. It wasn't locked. He pushed it open and stepped into the darkened hallway, gently closing the door behind him. He crept forward, keeping low, his torch focused on the floor giving him just enough light to take his next step without bumping into the wall.

The corridor was cold and smelled of a mixture of damp and disinfectant. He'd gone about fifteen metres when he heard the muffled voices. It sounded like a boy and a man. Colm and The Ghost? He was about to move closer when it struck him that this might be a very bad idea. What could he do? He needed numbers on his side if he was going to take on The Ghost. I may be Superdude, he thought, but this Ghost fella is some kind of Smartevildude. No, he'd better go back and make sure Lauryn had released the others – he couldn't believe his mother was actually here in a shopping centre in Dublin – and then they could storm the room. Between the lot of them they'd defeat The

Ghost, right? Although Seanie'd probably be a rubbish fighter. And the Drake fella had two broken hands, so he was out. Lauryn's mother? His mother? It wasn't like having Bruce Lee and Jackie Chan on your side, now was it? Still, what other choice did he have? He sighed as silently as he could, turned around and snuck back down the corridor.

He opened the door and stepped back into the main shopping area. The coast was clear. He just had to … wait a second. He swung the torch around. Right at the creature's eyes. The man who had once been Fintan Wickerly stared back at him. He didn't blink once in the harsh light.

'Uh-oh,' The Brute said. He snapped his hand forward, catching Wickerly on the chest with the butt of his torch. It had no effect.

'Uh-oh,' The Brute said again.

Wickerly reached out and grabbed him by the neck. The Brute felt the creature's thick fingers begin to tighten as it lifted him off the ground. He kicked out at Wickerly, catching him in an area that would have been considered vulnerable in most men. Not in Wickerly though.

The Brute's eyes began to bulge. He dropped the torch to the floor. It rolled along the ground, revealing another set of slow, shuffling feet. Then another, and another, until it came to a stop when it hit the rubbish bin outside Jammy's Newsagent.

Farther down the corridor he could hear a girl's scream. Lauryn, his mind echoed feebly as he began to weaken.

'Miiiiine,' rasped a voice.

Paddy the Bullkiller shuffled forward and swiped a huge hand in Wickerly's direction. He couldn't think clearly any more, but somehow Paddy knew that if he wanted to drain the life from the boy, he couldn't let this other creature have him. The hand connected with Wickerly's ear. It was enough to stun him momentarily. He dropped The Brute and turned towards the Bullkiller, lashing out in his slow, undead fashion.

The Brute shook his head clear. There was no time to waste, no time to retrieve the torch. He scrambled to his feet and set off, back towards Lauryn. He tripped over something in the darkness and went sprawling. Something fleshy grabbed at his face.

'Eeeeewwww, get off of me,' he yelled. He slapped

and kicked wildly until the flabby creature was knocked aside.

He was on his feet again, running. Running as fast as he could. He really was sick of running now. There was a light ahead. It was coming towards him.

'Lauryn?' he called out.

'Mikey?'

'Turn around. Zombies,' they both shouted at the same time.

They crashed into each other, knocking the last bit of wind out of themselves as they collapsed in a heap of arms and legs.

'There's a load of those undead after me,' The Brute said, leaping up.

Lauryn aimed the headlight over The Brute's shoulder. He was right. They were spread across the hallway, moving towards them with the shambling gait she'd grown to hate.

'It's no better on my side,' Lauryn said shining the lamp back in the direction she'd come from. More blank faces.

Her top was ripped at the shoulder, a little trickle of blood soaking into her black shirt.

'Can we break into one of those shops?' The Brute asked.

'I won't have time to pick the lock,' Lauryn said. 'What if we jump over the railing, down to the first floor?'

'Are you mad? Even if we survived we'd have so many broken bones we wouldn't be able to move. We'd just be lying there waiting for all those creatures to come along and finish us off,' The Brute said.

'Then it looks like we're trapped.'

She was right. Slowly the creatures came towards them from either side, like a group of bloodthirsty predators closing in on their prey.

Twenty-Five

'I f you help me complete my task,' The Ghost said, 'then I will save them all. You will die. That will not change, but you can save them. You're aware of how the creatures react to sunlight?'

Colm nodded, tears streaming down his face, his gaze still fixed on the monitors. His shoulders slumped in defeat. He was exhausted, drained, angry and terrified, but worst of all he was powerless to help his mother.

'These creatures are different. When you know how to use the keys you can command armies and eliminate their weaknesses. Regular light does not affect them, but I have had the most powerful industrial UV lights installed in all of the hallways. All you have to do is turn on the lights and the creatures will die and your family will be saved.'

'I don't believe you. Why would you install lights? You want those ghouls to stay alive.'

'Not when I am all-powerful. They'll be a hindrance to me then and I'll have to dispose of them quickly and simply.'

Without withdrawing his gaze from the scene unfolding before him, Colm replied, 'Why should I trust you?'

'You don't have to trust me. Once Abbatage starts, I will be frozen for a number of seconds. You can walk over and switch them on yourself.' The Ghost nodded towards the lighting control panel to his left. 'All you have to do is press the green button. But time is passing by and every second you waste puts your family in more danger. Tick tock.'

But I don't have to wait for the ritual, Colm thought. I can turn them on now. He rushed towards the lights, his fingers reaching for the switch. But before he knew what was happening he found himself lying on the ground, flat on his back, The Ghost's boot pressing into his chest.

'You didn't really think it would be that easy, did you?' The Ghost's attention was drawn by a frantic movement on one of the screens. 'Your mother looks terrified. The creature has almost broken through. In five minutes she'll be dead.'

Colm tried to wriggle free, but it was no use. The man was far too strong for him. He was trapped and it looked like there was no one coming to help him this time.

'All right, all right,' he said, defeated. 'I'll do what you want.'

The Ghost took his foot off Colm's chest and he scrambled to his feet.

The Ghost moved quickly. Time was running out for both of them. He grabbed Colm and dragged him to the centre of the room. It was more of an effort than it would have been in the past. His powers were weakening. His illness was beginning to consume him.

'Stand there. Do not move,' he said.

He opened a drawer in one of the desks and took out two iron manacles – rings with a length of chain attached. He fixed them to each of Colm's ankles in turn, snapping them shut. They were tight and they dug into the boy's skin. The Ghost drew out one of the lengths of chain and locked it onto a bolt on the door. Then he took the other and attached it to a bolt on the opposite wall. Both chains were taut and Colm realised he couldn't move his legs without falling over.

'I can't reach the light switch from here,' Colm said.

The Ghost didn't reply.

'Did you hear me? I can't reach the switch. How can I turn on the UV light?'

'You should have thought about that before you tried to trick me,' The Ghost said, as he emptied the keys into the palm of his hand. They emitted a bright light.

'I didn't trick you,' Colm cried.

'You tried to stop me from noticing that your friends had escaped.'

Lauryn and The Brute.

'You liar,' Colm shouted. 'You said I could trust you.' Even as he said the words he was aware of how stupid they were. What kind of person trusts an evil criminal?

One by one The Ghost placed the little diamonds into the slots in the shield.

Colm had never felt such hatred for anyone in his life. Suddenly his troubles with people like Ziggy and Buzzer seemed ridiculous. The hatred drove out his fear and he was filled with a sudden anger. He longed to take the shield and smash it over The Ghost's head again and again and again until he'd used up every last drop of energy, but he knew that he wasn't fast enough or strong enough. And he still had to save his family.

'I've changed my mind. I won't help you,' Colm said.

'Then they will all die.'

'If I can't move, I can't save them anyway.'

'If you don't help me, I will kill you now. If you do, then you still have time to find a way,' The Ghost said.

Find a way? How can I find a way? I've been so stupid, Colm thought. I've let him control everything and all I've done is sit around for the last eighteen months, waiting to be captured. There had to be something he could do, some way to save them ... even if it meant he had to die. For a moment his knees threatened to buckle. Die. The word echoed around his mind. He tried to block it out. Worry about that in a minute. Save them first, then worry about trying to save yourself.

'It's time,' The Ghost said.

·◆·

Cedric and Kate had tried their best to break out of the

shop, but no matter what they threw at the front door – a chair, a till, a counter – the glass wouldn't smash. It had cracked, even wobbled slightly, but it wouldn't break. Kate had been disappointed to find that, for a detective, Cedric's lock-picking skills were almost non-existent.

'You know, if we get out of here, I'm going to get that glass installed in my office. No burglar could get through that,' Cedric had said.

Kate hadn't been listening to him. She was hopping mad.

'Ced, I just want to get out there, find those kidnapping zombies and give them a huge bear hug. I'm going to squeeze them so tight their heads are going to pop off.'

'If we're going to get out of here, we're going to have to find another way. I've got an idea.'

That light bulb-over-the-head moment was the reason they were now crawling on their hands and knees through the air duct system which wound its way across the top of the shopping centre, hidden from the public below by flimsy white ceiling tiles. It was a tight squeeze. Cedric led the way, slowly moving forward, desperately hoping that he wouldn't encounter one of the creatures. There was no way he was going to be able to turn around and crawl away – his head and shoulders were brushing the roof of the duct as it was – and with Kate behind him, well, best not to think about what might happen until it actually did.

Kate was growing increasingly claustrophobic. After the time she'd spent in her wooden prison, the last thing she needed was to feel trapped again.

'Can't you move any faster, Cedric Murphy?'

'I'm doing the best I can,' Cedric huffed as he wriggled his way forward.

'Well, do better. My nose is practically up your bum.'

'I …' His words caught in his throat.

'What is it?' Kate whispered, her apprehension growing.

'It's OK. I thought it was one of those creatures, but it's not.'

'That's a relief,' Kate said.

'Yeah, it's just a couple of rats.'

Kate began to shriek. So did Cedric.

·◆·

The Brute and Lauryn weren't going to go down without a fight. Luckily for them, the undead weren't organised enough to converge on the teenagers all at once. If they had done, then they would have been overpowered in seconds. As it was, fighting them off one by one was taking its toll. Every kick Lauryn executed, every punch The Brute threw was effective, but it was tiring them out rapidly. They were drenched in sweat, their arms and legs aching with the effort, but they fought on. The teenagers kept knocking the creatures down, but they kept getting to their feet again.

'Back to back,' Lauryn said.

The Brute understood what she meant. If they stood that way, they could see the creatures approaching from all sides. They moved in unison, ducking beneath the creatures' hands, sweeping their legs from under them. Fists crunched as they connected with cartilage and bone. Bodies thudded to the ground. Some of the creatures went down silently, others with a sound like cattle lowing. But they never stopped coming.

Above the noise, The Brute heard the rasping deathly voices of Paddy the Bullkiller and Wickerly as they moved ever nearer. They were the strongest of them all. He didn't know if he had it in him to defeat them, but he wasn't going to let Lauryn know that.

'I think we're winning,' he spluttered as he drew some air into his gasping lungs.

'If this is us winning, I'd hate to see what losing's like,' Lauryn said as she smashed one of the undead in the knee.

'Still trying to be positive,' The Brute said. He swung wildly and hit fresh air. His timing was going.

There was a loud cracking noise above them. The ceiling tiles began to shake.

'What was that?' Lauryn asked.

'Dunno, just keep fighting.'

·◆·

'Turn around, Kate.'

'I hate rats!'

'I hate them more.'

Kate managed to partially turn, but then found herself tightly wedged in the duct. She frantically twisted her body left and right. She had to get away. But it was no good. She was just wedging herself in tighter.

'Where are they?'

'I can't see them any more,' Cedric called out. 'Aaargghh. One of them just ran up my leg.'

'Eeeeeewwwww,' Kate shrieked. 'He's touching me. He's on my leg. Get off, get off, get off.'

'Aaaarggh. Stop pinching so hard. That's not a rat, that's my hand.'

The duct began to swing to and fro, gently at first, but gaining momentum every time Kate and Cedric moved. There was a huge creak.

'Ced?'

'Brace yourself, Kate, I think we're going to fall.'

The rivets holding the metal together popped one by one in a matter of seconds. There was a brief moment when Cedric thought it was OK, that by some miracle they were going to remain suspended in the air, but it was only a brief moment. Then they came crashing down.

• ◆ •

Lauryn thought the world was falling in when the ceiling tiles exploded and the two large dark shapes plummeted towards the ground. Kate and Cedric's falls were broken by four of the unfortunate creatures.

'What the–' The Brute began.

'Hey, it's that guy from the house and Kate Whatshername,' Lauryn said as the detecting duo slowly got to their feet. 'Look out,' she called, as Wickerly lumbered towards Kate.

Kate had seen him. 'Come to Momma,' she yelled. She grabbed the creature around the waist and lifted him into the air. Wickerly failed to understand what was happening; he just knew something wasn't right. He snapped his jaws at her, but she easily evaded his bite. She just squeezed and squeezed until all the fight began to leave Wickerly. She flung him against the railing and he slithered to the ground in a jelly-like heap.

'Did that really just happen?' The Brute asked, looking at Kate in awe.

'Come on, kids. Let's kick some zombie ass,' Cedric shouted, flat-palming a creature in the face.

'Told you, Mikey – we ain't beaten yet,' Lauryn said as she threw herself at one of the undead.

·◆·

The Ghost took off his coat and dropped it to the ground. He rolled up the sleeves of his shirt revealing tattoos of the Sign of Lazarus – the little diamond with the skull at its centre. There was one on the inside of each arm, just above the wrist. He removed his hat. Colm gasped when he saw the crudely inked tattoo in the middle of the man's forehead. It had jagged edges and wept tiny drops of blood, as if the job had been done only recently, and very hurriedly.

'If you don't follow my instructions closely, I will use an override switch to automatically unlock all the doors in this building, allowing the undead to roam free and kill at will. Whatever chance your friends and family still have will be extinguished immediately. Do you understand?'

Colm nodded.

'Pick up the shield,' The Ghost commanded.

Colm did as he was told. The shield trembled in his hands.

The Ghost took two paces backwards. He stood less than three metres away from Colm, directly facing him.

'Raise the shield until its face is pointing towards me.'

Colm's fingers gripped the edge of the wooden shield and he lifted it into the air. His mind was racing. He knew he had to act now, but he had no idea what to do. What could he do? Hydrochloric acid had half-destroyed the last key, but he couldn't just pry one out of the shield and swallow it. The man would be too fast for him. Anyway, how stupid would that be? He didn't know what damage that would do to him and he wasn't going to be able to help anyone if he was in a withered heap on the ground.

Maybe he could just spit on the keys? If there was acid was in his stomach and his stomach was connected to his mouth then it must be in his saliva too. It sort of made sense, but ... if the acid was in his saliva then there'd be no teeth or tongue left in his mouth – they'd have worn away years ago.

'I am the last of the Sign of Lazarus,' The Ghost whispered.

He stretched his arms out wide, away from his body, until the tattoos were facing the shield. The keys began to sparkle and spin around within the centrepiece. The light increased until nothing seemed to exist in the room other than Colm, the shield and the criminal. The Ghost's face became serene. He closed his eyes. A man ready to receive his destiny.

The life force began to drain from Colm. It was

similar to the feeling he'd had the previous year when he'd held one key in his hand. But this was stronger, more powerful. His thoughts began to drift, and strange images filled his head – things he'd seen, people he'd known, places he'd been. Long forgotten nightmares resurfaced. He began to weaken. He tried to shake off the feeling, to get back to reality.

He heard far-distant screams and glanced towards the monitor. The undead were swarming around The Brute and Lauryn. And Cedric and Kate? Was that them? His mother was trying to escape the clutches of one of the hideous creatures. There was too much happening all at once. Too much to think about.

The shield shuddered in his hands. What if he threw it to the ground? Would that do any good? Would it stop the … it was too late. The time for thinking was over. The shield shook violently. The light grew brighter. Harsher.

A key shot forward from the shield like a missile. Almost faster than the eye could take in. One moment it was there, the next it had disappeared. Colm blinked. Where had it gone? It was only when he heard The Ghost cry out that he realised what had happened.

He looked at his enemy. There it was – embedded in the man's wrist. At that velocity it should have torn through his arm and out the other side, yet it hadn't. It was stuck in the pale flesh, right in the tattoo of the Sign of Lazarus. The light from the key spread along the arm as the veins just beneath the skin rose to the surface and started to pulse. The Ghost's body began to absorb the diamond, the object becoming part of him.

It was really happening.

Colm tried to twist the shield away from the man, but he wasn't strong enough. It was as if it had taken on a life of its own and was communicating directly with The Ghost. It was part of the ceremony too.

The second key flew through the air and landed on the tattoo on the other arm. There was a short popping sound as it was sucked into the flesh, but this was drowned out when The Ghost cried out again, louder this time. He struggled to keep his arms aloft. His mouth began to foam.

There was only one key left. And Colm hadn't a clue what to do. He tried to let his mind relax, to stop the bad words from clouding his brain, words like weakness, sickness, pain, death. But his energy was still fading away.

The final Lazarus Key began to spin faster and faster within the shield. Colm's key. In seconds it would launch itself forward until it thudded into the third tattoo on The Ghost's forehead. The ceremony would be complete and The Ghost would become immortal.

The shield cracked. Splinters of wood fell to the floor. The room began to shake. The fluorescent light shattered.

Without really understanding what he was doing, Colm let his right hand drop free of the shield, taking all the weight in his left. He placed his hand in front of the key, where he imagined the centrepiece should be, just as it launched itself forward.

He felt an enormous surge of pain as the final Lazarus Key ripped through his hand, leaving a gaping hole in his palm.

It was enough to deflect the key from its target.

It zipped through the air, centimetres higher than it should have been. It scraped along the top of The Ghost's head, leaving a trail of blood, and hit the wall.

The Ghost's eyes snapped open. The shield clattered to the ground.

Colm could hardly believe it. He'd done it. He'd stopped the ceremony.

'I'll kill you,' The Ghost roared, rushing forward.

Colm tried to turn and run, but the chains pulled him back and he fell to the floor. When he looked up, The Ghost was standing above him, gripped by a terrible fury. Colm had never seen anyone look so angry in his life and terror surged through him.

He had stopped the Abbatage, but he hadn't stopped The Ghost.

He was a dead boy. He knew it.

But as the man reached for him, something began to change. The Ghost noticed it before Colm did. His mouth twisted in pain. He looked at his arms, where the keys had buried themselves.

They began to spark.

The skull within the diamond seemed to grow larger and the white surface was suddenly engulfed in flames. Trails of smoke curled around the man's pale arms.

'What's happening to me?' he asked.

Colm didn't have an answer.

The smoke began to twist itself into a shape. Something dark and menacing.

This was bad. This was very bad. Colm shut his eyes.

When he heard The Ghost scream he opened them again.

There was a figure in the room. A smoky figure dressed in clothing from another time. Centuries ago.

The figure spoke in a quiet, whispery voice. A language that Colm had never heard before. Its nails were long and pointed. The Ghost's eyes widened as the figure leaped on him and began to feed. He tried to fight back, but he couldn't get a grip on this new creature. It was like fighting fog.

The smoke continued to pour from his arms and twisted itself into other shapes.

As more and more emerged and began to feed on The Ghost, Colm started to understand what was happening. The life force of everyone who had ever held the keys that were embedded in The Ghost's arms was reforming and consuming him. Attila the Hun. Vlad the Impaler. Generations of warriors. The Ghost flailed wildly, lashing out, trying to connect with what wasn't there. He had killed many people, but this was an enemy he couldn't defeat.

Colm began to cough and choke on the acrid smoke

as the room became crowded with more and more ancient figures and The Ghost's screams grew louder and louder. They were seeking revenge for the life that had been stolen from them and their bloodthirsty roars and gleeful feeding were too much for Colm to take. As The Ghost began to wither and his movements grew more desperate, Colm shut his eyes again.

He didn't open them until the screaming had stopped.

A thick fog of smoke hung in the air. Colm's eyes stung and watered. He was shaking. He glanced around, expecting one of the figures to attack him, but the room was empty. They had all disappeared. So had The Ghost. All that was left of him were the two keys lying on the ground. They didn't glow any longer. They were dull and lifeless now, as if their time was over.

Was it over, Colm wondered? Why hadn't they taken him? Was it because the keys were in ... he heard a scream in the distance and for a moment his heart raced and he expected to be attacked.

'Mam and Dad,' he said. He'd almost forgotten them.

They were still in danger. He could worry about all that had happened later. He had to save them. But how? He was still a prisoner.

He got to his feet, the chains tugging at his ankles. He didn't feel good. It was as if something was changing within him. Waves of nausea swept over him. He pulled at the manacles, but there was no way to open them now. Not quickly anyway. He tried to wrench the chains from the wall, but that didn't work either. They were bolted on too well. There had to be something he could do. Some way he could turn on those UV lights and destroy the creatures out there. There was nothing useful within reach except the shield.

'Well, that's going to have to do,' Colm said.

The smoke began to clear and he could see the monitors again. His mother was still alive. His dad too. There was still time.

He held his torn right hand against his side and stretched his left as far as he could, trying to grab the shield. His fingers grazed the edge of it, but just pushed it farther away. His face grew red with the effort, even as the rest of him felt icy cold. At this angle, he realised, it would be easier to get to if he used his right hand. Once again he stretched out and this time his fingers curled around the edge of the wooden shield.

'Yes,' he shouted as he got a grip.

He dragged it towards him. It scraped the bloodied hole in his hand. The pain was excruciating. Everything turned white and blank and for a moment he was calm. Then he shook himself and returned to a world of blinding pain. The shield was sticky with his blood. He was on the verge of passing out, but something inside him refused to give in.

He stood up and held the shield in both hands.

He looked over to where the green button was. About two and a half metres away. He'd always been useless at any sporting activity, but this was one time he was going to have to excel. He was only going to get one shot at it.

He twisted his body around like a discus thrower and took a practice swing. The wooden implement was heavy. He wasn't sure how far he could …

'Ah, stop thinking and just do it, you eejit,' he said as he flung the shield forward.

He held his breath as it arced through the air.

It crashed down on the button.

On the monitors he saw a blinding flash as the lights burst into life all over the shopping centre.

And then he collapsed.

Twenty-Six

Colm woke up in the back of a stationary ambulance in the shopping centre's car park. There wasn't a part of him that didn't ache. He was lying on a trolley and when he sat up, waves of pain surged through his body. His right hand was wrapped in white bandages. The back doors of the ambulance were open and he peered out into the morning sunshine. He could see his mother and father talking to a paramedic. He forgot about the pain for a moment. They were alive. He'd saved them. His mam and dad.

There were garda cars everywhere and people milling about, most of them looking like they were in a hurry. He saw The Brute and Lauryn. Lauryn's mother.

Cedric Murphy. Kate Finkle. He'd saved them too.

He tried to remember what had happened. Had The Ghost really been destroyed? He'd seen it with his own eyes. It had happened, hadn't it? And the keys? He hadn't destroyed them. Someone could still use them. He had to find them. If he had them then no one else could ... had to go back to the control room ... find them. He tried to stand up, but another wave of pain hit him. He fell back onto the trolley.

Everything was a blur after that.

Fragments.

Concerned voices. Sirens. Hospital corridors and sleep. Lots and lots of sleep.

In and out of consciousness.

People visiting him in hospital.

His parents crying.

His grandparents standing helplessly at his bedside clutching bottles of Lucozade.

The Brute carrying a bunch of flowers.

Someone showing him a newspaper with a headline saying The Ghost was dead.

A nurse shooing away reporters.

The light hurting his eyes.

The pain when a nurse opened the blinds.

And finally, a darkened room.

·◆·

He woke up to find Professor Peter Drake sitting at his bedside, a worried look on his face. When he saw Colm was awake he tried to smile, but it didn't come out right.

'How are you feeling?' he asked.

'Great,' Colm lied.

His arms were covered in bandages and there were wires and tubes attached to his chest and nose. His skin had begun to turn a shade of purple.

'You don't look that good,' the professor said.

'What's happening to me?' Colm asked.

'You won't like it.'

Professor Drake was an expert on the history of the Lazarus Keys and the only one who was even close to understanding what Colm had gone through.

'Tell me anyway.'

'From what I've been able to uncover, you're undergoing a transformation. Does the light hurt your eyes?'

'Yes,' Colm replied.

'Do you feel more tetchy? Do you get angry a little quicker than you used to?'

'Yes.'

'Are you hungry all the time?'

'Definitely,' Colm said.

Professor Drake nodded. He took a cigarette case from the inside pocket of his blazer. He fumbled at the little silver box with his broken, bandaged fingers.

'You can't smoke in here, Professor.'

'What? Oh right, regulations and all that. My apologies.'

An uncomfortable silence developed.

'I'm going to become one of them, aren't I? One of the undead,' Colm said.

'Yes. As best we can determine, yes. But we don't know for sure. That was the first time the Abbatage has been performed in hundreds of years. The first time it's been interrupted too, obviously. We don't know the full consequences. You are the guinea pig in this experiment.'

'So I could become a creature of the night?' Colm asked.

'Yes.'

'Or I could wake up with superpowers?'

The professor smiled properly for the first time. 'Less likely, but anything's possible. Unfortunately, in one sense only, the person who truly knew how the keys worked is, well, very, very dead.'

'Did you find anything ...'

'Actually, yes, we found a small notebook written in code. Our best people are attempting to decipher it even as we speak.'

'That's good, Professor.'

Colm closed his eyes for a moment.

'Don't tell anyone, but I'm a bit scared.'

'No one can blame you for that. But don't give up hope yet. We have people working night and day on a cure. And you have some unlikely, but resourceful allies.'

'Professor, I never give up,' Colm said as he drifted into a dreamless sleep.

Twenty-Seven

C edric hadn't been looking forward to driving the damaged rental car to Shannon airport, so he'd been putting it off for two days. He had a feeling that when Mark had asked him to return it in pristine condition, he hadn't meant with a broken windscreen, bald tyres, three minor dents to the bodywork, two major ones, damaged paintwork and the cigar burn that Kate had left on the car seat when they'd finally driven home after the night in the shopping centre. He knew he was in trouble too if the large number of increasingly irate voicemails Mark had left on his phone was anything to go by. Still, that problem could wait until later. Now that he was sitting here on Kate's ratty couch, he was happier than he'd been in a very long time.

'So, is that it? Is the whole thing finally over?' Kate asked, interrupting his thoughts, as she shooed Mr Gilchrist away with her foot.

'Yes, definitely,' Cedric replied emphatically.

'Yeah, I seem to remember you saying that once before. You were wrong.'

'OK.'

'Very wrong.'

'I said OK,' Cedric snapped.

'The Ghost is dead, right?' Kate said. She took a long drag on her Cuban cigar. Man, I missed these babies, she thought. 'Really dead?'

'He's dead,' Cedric said. 'Scout's honour.'

'Just wanted to make sure,' Kate said.

A fog of smoke, thick and almost impenetrable, wafted towards the ceiling.

'And before you ask,' Cedric continued, 'Professor Drake and a bunch of UCD scientists dropped the remnants of the shield and the Lazarus Keys into a giant vat of deadly hydrochloric acid, then sealed it in some sort of lead before burying it somewhere secret.'

'And that should have destroyed them?'

'No, it would have given them a nice little polish so now they're all shiny and new. Of course it destroyed them. Drake is an expert and he's certain that only three ever existed. One from the Red House Hotel and the other two. One plus two makes three.'

'Very clever. Good to know you can count, Mr Patronising. See how many fingers I'm holding up? It's less than three,' Kate said.

'Oh, that's charming,' Cedric said, glancing over. 'Very ladylike.'

'I'm glad to see that wiry fella and the others got their comeuppance.'

'Me too,' Cedric agreed. 'Maybe being blown to smithereens was a bit of a harsh punishment though.'

'No way,' Kate said. 'Anyone involved in the kidnap of innocent people deserves what's coming to them.'

'Glad you don't run the country with that attitude. Anyway, with The Ghost a goner, The Ark Detective Agency he opened to ruin our business will be closed down. Which means things will soon be back to normal for the Murphy & Finkle Detective Agency,' Cedric said.

'Murphy & Finkle? You're making me a partner?'

'I think it's about time, don't you? Wait. Are you

actually crying?'

'No. Shut up,' Kate said, giving Cedric a thump on the shoulder with one hand and wiping away a tear with the other.

'Ow. You know, you look really classy with your streaming nose and the cigar clamped between your teeth like that.'

'I'm rubber you're glue. Whatever you say bounces off of me and sticks to you.'

'Very mature, Kate. Very mature. I'm already reconsidering offering you that partnership.'

She ignored the jibe.

'So this Ghost lad, what do you think his plan was? He never actually told anyone,' Kate said.

'I've been thinking about that a lot. He wanted to pay back anyone who happened to be at the Red House Hotel the night his brother died, so he got those thugs to destroy my business, caused Colm's father to lose his job and a whole lot of other stuff. But, according to what the others are saying, he must have changed his mind for some reason. He didn't care about destroying us any more, he just wanted to become immortal.'

'Maybe he was dying or something,' Kate said.

'Nah, I doubt it,' Cedric said, not realising that Kate had actually hit the nail on the head.

'You're probably right. You're better at this figuring out stuff than I am.'

'That's why my name's going to be first on our letterheads,' Cedric said.

'I'm impressed that you managed to work it all out.'

'Thank you,' Cedric replied, beaming with pride.

'Of course, I'd have been more impressed if you figured it out *before* it happened and stopped a lot of needless kidnapping and zombie fighting. Seems to me like that's what a proper detective would have done.'

'Shut up, Kate.'

'You wouldn't catch Sherlock Holmes letting the criminals get away with taking him hostage, locking him up in a shop, and only coming to his conclusions when it was all done and dusted and the bad guys were dead.'

'I said: shut up, Kate.'

Cedric looked at her. As the early morning light streamed through the dusty curtains, after all they'd been through, she'd never looked more lovely to him. Her thick fringe of hair nestled on her bushy eyebrows, and a smile – or the delayed reaction from the onion rings she'd eaten for breakfast – played on her lips. She was almost beautiful.

The doorbell rang, interrupting the moment.

'I'll be back in a second,' Kate said.

He heard the front door creak open. This was followed by the sound of excited voices. Young voices. Teenage voices. Oh no, not them, Cedric thought.

Kate ushered The Brute and Lauryn into the living room. Cedric didn't bother to get up.

'You two? How did you find us?' he asked.

'You're not the only detective–' Lauryn began.

'Kate invited us over … oh, right, you were trying to make us look good,' The Brute said.

'Yeah, thanks for that, Mikey,' Lauryn said, giving him a withering look.

'Do you two want a drink or something to eat?' Kate asked.

Lauryn glanced around the apartment. It wasn't the type of place that was likely to win any hygiene awards. 'No thanks,' she said. She wasn't even sure if she'd be happy sitting down on the couch. It looked like it came from a dump.

'Shouldn't you be in school?' Cedric asked.

'Mid-term break,' The Brute replied.

'Fantastic. I'm delighted for you. Kate, can I have a word,' Cedric asked.

'It's OK, Ced. There's a reason I invited them over. A reason I invited you over too,' Kate said.

'It wasn't just because of my natural charm and amazing conversational skills?' Cedric asked, pretending to be surprised. 'You know, if I had known these two were turning up, I wouldn't have called over. I have a lot to do. I'm a busy man.'

'You're sitting in your friend's flat on a Tuesday morning,' The Brute said. 'How busy can you be?'

Kate suppressed a snigger.

'We need your help,' Lauryn said. 'You heard about Colm, right? He's sick.'

'Yeah, I heard. Sorry,' Cedric said. 'But I'm not a doctor, so I don't think—'

'That's not the kind of help we need. What Colm has, well, let's just say traditional medicine isn't likely to provide a cure. According to the Prof, we have about three days to save him,' Lauryn said. 'And we're going to save him, right?'

'I still don't see what this has to do with me.'

'We need a detective,' The Brute said.

'For what?'

'Remember when the UV light came on and destroyed all the undead that night in the shopping centre?' Lauryn asked.

'No, why don't you jog my memory?' Cedric said.

'Wow, you're so sarcastic. How do you put up with him, Kate?'

'I'm a saint,' Kate replied, belching a smoke ring.

'Back to your reason for coming here,' Cedric said, tapping his watch.

'Right. The UV light didn't destroy every member of the undead. One of them survived it. We don't know why, but the Prof reckons that we may be able to save Colm if we can figure out how this guy survived when all the others didn't. At the very least we'll be able to buy him more time,' Lauryn said.

'And you need me because ...'

'He's disappeared. We need to find him and fast.' Lauryn handed him a photo. It was a screen grab from the CCTV footage. 'That's the guy we need to find.'

Cedric looked at the picture of Fintan Wickerly.

'You want me to go zombie hunting?'

'Technically, he's not a zombie ...' The Brute began.

'I don't care what he is. I'm not going to help you. Every time I meet you two it means trouble for me and this time I'm putting my foot down and saying: No Way José. Not on your Nelly. Count me out.'

There was a rumble as Kate cleared her throat loudly. Cedric looked over at her. 'I'm helping them, aren't I?'

'Oh yeah.'

'Fine. Let's get our coats. It's time to go to work,' Cedric sighed.

Also available from Mercier Press

COLM & THE LAZARUS KEY

Kieran Mark Crowley

ISBN: 978 1 85635 646 6

Colm thinks that spending a fortnight with his cousin – The Brute –
is the worst thing that can happen to him. He's about to find out he's
wrong. Very wrong.

While driving The Brute home, Colm and his parents stop for the
night at a quiet, old hotel. Then Colm finds *The Book of Dread* and sets
off a chain of events that lands him right in the middle of an adventure,
whether he wants to be or not. Colm and The Brute must overcome
their dislike of each other and work together if they're going to defeat
the evil criminal and the monstrous creature who both hope to claim
the Lazarus Key and use it to take over the world.

Also available from Mercier Press

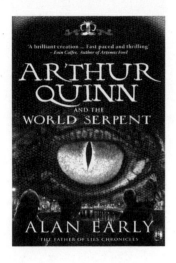

ARTHUR QUINN AND THE WORLD SERPENT

Alan Early

ISBN: 978 1 85635 827 9

Arthur Quinn has problems. He has just moved to Dublin and started a new school, and now he's having crazy dreams about the Viking god Loki. But it soon becomes clear these are more than dreams – Arthur is actually having premonitions about a great evil that threatens the world.

With his new friends, Will and Ash, Arthur sets out to discover what Loki is up to. Together they discover that under the streets of Dublin, buried in a secret chamber, is a creature that's been imprisoned for a thousand years, a creature that can and will destroy the world if Loki has anything to do with it.

www.mercierpress.ie

Also available from Mercier Press

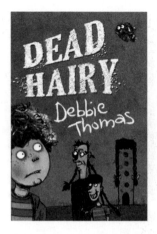

Dead Hairy

Debbie Thomas

ISBN: 978 1 85635 678 7

Welcome to the Hair Museum, where history has hairdos and
fish have beards …

When Squashy Grandma's teeth get stuck in the vacuum cleaner,
Abbie Hartley calls the Very Odd Job Man. He arrives with his wacky
daughter Perdita. Adventurous Abbie is thrilled when Perdita asks
for help in the search for her mum Coriander, who has disappeared
mysteriously. But waddling in the shadows is the burger-shaped villain
Dr Hubris Klench. How can Abbie help to save Coriander – not to
mention the world – from Klench's 'eefil doinks'?

Full of laughs and lice crispies, *Dead Hairy* will delight children,
parents and squashy grandmas alike.

www.mercierpress.ie

Also available from Mercier Press

THE LEGEND SERIES
BY TOM MCCAUGHREN

THE LEGEND OF THE GOLDEN KEY

978 1 85635 803 3

Tapser and his cousin Cowlick set out to solve the mystery of the missing treasure of the King family, and are soon caught up in a race against dangerous adversaries to find the gold before it is lost forever.

THE LEGEND OF THE PHANTOM HIGHWAYMAN

978 1 85635 802 6

Tapser and his cousins Cowlick, Rachel and Róisín get caught up in a tangled web of ghost riders, smugglers and spies when they try to solve the mystery of Hugh Rua, the phantom highwayman.

THE LEGEND OF THE CORRIB KING

978 1 85635 801 9

Tapser and his cousins must decipher a puzzle in the form of a poem to find their missing Uncle Pakie before it is too late.

www.mercierpress.ie